SEX IN
DUBLIN

EDITED BY

MAXIM JAKUBOWSKI

Published by Accent Press Ltd – 2010

ISBN 9781907016233

Printed and bound in the UK

Cover design by
Zipline Creative

Contents

Introduction

I AM RELIABLY INFORMED that the art and practice of sex is well-known outside of major cities too, but that's another book altogether!

Our new SEX IN THE CITY series is devoted to the unique attraction that major cities worldwide provide to lovers of all things erotic. Famous places and monuments, legendary streets and avenues, unforgettable landmarks all conjugate with our memories of loves past and present, requited and unrequited, to form a map of the heart like no other. Brief encounters, long-lasting affairs and relationships, the glimpse of a face, of hidden flesh, eyes in a crowd, everything about cities can be sexy, naughty, provocative, dangerous and exciting.

Cities are not just about monuments and museums and iconic places, they are also about people at love and play in unique surroundings. With this in mind, these anthologies of erotica will imaginatively explore the secret stories of famous cities and bring them to life, by unveiling passion and love, lust and sadness, glittering flesh and sexual temptation, the art of love and a unique sense of place.

And we thought it would be a good idea to invite some of the best writers not only of erotica, but also from the mainstream and even the crime and mystery field, to offer us specially written new stories about the hidden side of some of our favourite cities, to reveal what happens behind closed doors (and sometimes even in public). And they have delivered in trumps.

The stories you are about to read cover the whole spectrum from young love to forbidden love and every sexual variation in between. Funny, harrowing, touching, sad, joyful, every human emotion is present and how could it not be when sex and the delights of love are evoked so skilfully?

Our initial batch of four volumes takes us to London, New York, Paris and Dublin, all cities with a fascinating attraction to matters of the flesh and the heart. We hope you read them all and begin to collect them, and that we shall soon be offering you further excursions to the wild shores of erotic Los Angeles, Venice, Edinburgh, New Orleans, Sydney, Tokyo, Berlin, Rio, Moscow, Barcelona and beyond. Our authors are all raring to go and have already packed their imagination so they can offer you more sexy thrills …

And it's cheaper than a plane ticket!

So, come and enjoy sex in the city.

Maxim Jakubowski

Dublin Express
by Colin Bateman

DANNY GUTHRIE SAID, 'EXCUSE me, is this seat taken?'

Her eyes flitted up. She had dark hair and pale skin with a reddish tinge; was maybe twenty. College books out on the table, iPod earphones and the *tsk-tsk* of her music. This train, the Dublin train, was far from packed. It was mid-morning, spring. He'd got on at Drogheda and patrolled up and down the corridor until he spotted her.

She didn't really say yes or no, just nodded, which could have meant anything. But he sat and she returned her attention to her books. He tried to read them upside down.

He said, 'French?'

She said, 'What?' and pulled out one of her earphones.

'Studying French?' She nodded. Before she could put it back in he said, 'You must have exams coming up, studying on a Saturday.'

'Yeah. Soon.' She replaced the earphone. Her cheeks were a little redder. She was easily embarrassed.

'That's good,' he said. 'If it needs doing.'

She looked up. 'Sorry?' She pulled the earphone out again.

'Sorry, didn't mean to disturb you.'

'No, it's OK.' It clearly *wasn't* OK, but now she felt she couldn't just go back to the music. 'What were you

3

saying?'

'Nothing, really. Just … French, it's a beautiful language.'

'Oh. Do you …?'

'*Oui.*'

He smiled, and she smiled, getting it. He was a bit older than her: short black hair, hint of stubble. Neat.

'You going into town?' he asked.

Stupid question; just for the sake of it really. Of course she was going into town. The train was going into town; it was an express, no other stops between Drogheda and town.

'Oh, yeah. Yeah. Meeting my boyfriend.'

Making a point. *Boyfriend.* When he held her gaze she managed a half smile, then looked away. Banks of unsold apartments slid past. He watched them as well.

Then she said, 'You?'

'Yeah. Into town. Something to do. *Man on a mission.*'

'Mysterious.'

'Yeah, kinda.'

'You could tell me, but then you'd have to kill me?'

But he didn't smile back the way she expected; he just kept looking at her. She felt a bit foolish and averted her eyes. She didn't know him from Adam. He could easily be a nutter. She looked up again, and *now* he was smiling. He was full of himself. She quite liked that, in a man.

Danny Guthrie said, 'You're not going to see the President?'

'The President?'

'Aye. She's giving a speech out at the Barracks. Anniversary of something or other.'

'No. No interest.'

'Funny that, isn't it? If it was the President of like, America, there'd be motorcades and Secret Service and

4

all that shit. But with her, you know, she'll be lucky if there's a traffic warden and a guard with a dodgy walkie-talkie. President of our own country, nobody gives a toss.'

'Yeah, yeah, I suppose. But I mean, she's ceremonial more than … you know? She doesn't have her finger on the nuclear button or anything.'

'Yeah, I suppose. I'm going to pop out anyway, have a listen.'

'Really?'

'Sure. Like I said. *Man on a mission.*'

This time he patted his jacket.

She gave a little laugh, but at the same time her brow furrowed. She pretended to pat her blouse, like what's the big secret? But he just kept looking at her. She pretended to return her attention to her books. Without quite looking up she was aware that he was closer, arms folded, on the table, leaning towards her.

Danny Guthrie said: 'Do you think if someone has the chance to alter the course of history, for the good, they should?'

'I'm sorry?'

'Do you … I mean, look you're studying French, right? Say if a couple of hundred years ago someone, say a waiter, had had the foresight to whisper in Napoleon's ear that invading Russia was really going to fuck him up. And in so whispering, and Napoleon taking it on board, he saved the lives of hundreds of thousands of soldiers, do you think you would have whispered, if you were a waiter, waitress? Or would you have said, these big world events have nothing to do with me, I just serve frog's legs and shit?'

'If I was a just a waitress, how would I even know what could happen during a Russian campaign?'

'Well, for one, I think you're needlessly complicating

5

this, but for the sake of argument: you're a waitress whose family came from Russia, and you know how bloody cold the winters are, which a lot of people in France at the time must have known too, but were too bloody scared to say. At least until you came along. But my point is, do you think you would have said something?'

'Well, I'd like to think so.'

'OK, but what if we took it one step further. Say Lee Harvey Oswald ...'

'Lee Harvey Oswald.'

He started to look exasperated, but his frustration was halted by her sudden, radiant smile. 'Sorry,' she said.

It was good that she was more relaxed with him now, bearing in mind what was coming. 'You know the story, OK? He was in the Book Depository. But say he was getting set up to shoot Kennedy, and you happened to walk in and say, 'Lee Harvey Oswald, what do you think you're doing?' And he said he was going to shoot the President because of the Bay of Pigs and the Mafia, or whatever, but now you knew what he was planning, so he was going to have to kill you, and you knew it too, and he knew that you knew it, so you had a choice to make. You could either run for it, which wasn't going to work, or start screaming. But who was going to hear you way up there with all the noise outside, waiting for the President? So what would you do? You wanted to save your own life, and you wanted to save the President's, so what really would you do?'

'I ... don't know.'

'What have you got to bargain with?'

'I don't ... I'm not sure what you mean.'

'There's this guy in front of you. He's like an ex-marine or something, so he's built. But he's also a bit

6

nerdy looking, and you, you're this young girl, young beautiful student, how're you going to distract him? And save the President, maybe save the world, because the fingers on nuclear buttons could easily press fire if Kennedy goes down? What're you going to do?'

'I don't really …'

'Would you do it?'

'Would I do what?'

'Would you say to Lee Harvey Oswald, on the verge of maybe destroying civilisation as we know it, would you say: Lee Harvey, you can make love to me right now, if only you won't do this terrible thing. And afterwards I promise I won't even tell a single person what you were up to.'

'You mean would I have sex with him?'

'To save the world.'

'I don't know. God. Why would you ever ask such a … Yes. Maybe. To save the world.' She was very flushed now. 'He'd have to wear a condom.'

Danny Guthrie said, 'What if that was a deal-breaker?'

'Wearing a condom?'

'Yes, what if he had a strict no condoms rule?'

'Well, yes, maybe to save the world. God. How did we start talking about this? We're nearly in town.'

'It's just interesting, isn't it? So, if you'll forgive my French, if we zipped back forty, fifty years, to save the President, Camelot, all that bollocks, you would screw Lee Harvey Oswald on the floor of the Texas Book Depository.'

'The floor?'

'Yes. The floor.'

'I suppose. To save the world.'

'OK then, obvious next question. Say the equivalent of Lee Harvey Oswald, a twenty-first century Lee Harvey,

7

got on this train, and he was on his way to assassinate, say, the President of Ireland, what would you do to save her?'

'Well it's hardly the same thing, is it?'

'OK, granted, no it's not. Obviously she hasn't got that same standing. Nobody hangs on her every word. But for the sake of argument, if you could save her life, what would you do? If someone who got on a train and sat down beside you and said they were going to shoot the President of Ireland, but might not if you agreed to ride them in the toilets?'

'No,' she said.

'Not just to save the life of the President of this country, but to save the life of a person? Of a *woman*?'

'No.'

'No? Why not?'

'Because doing that and saving the world, there's a big difference between doing it and saving one person. Horrible choice as it is, I wouldn't.'

'What would you do?'

'In what sense?'

'In a sexual sense.'

'To save the President of Ireland what would I do in a sexual sense?'

'Yes.' He patted his jacket. 'If he, the lunatic with the gun in his coat said to you, show me one of your breasts right here, right now, and I won't take the head off the President of this green and pleasant land, would you do it?'

'Do you have a gun in your jacket?'

'Oh, we're talking about me, are we? Are you sure about that? And if we are, do I have a gun? Well, that's for you to decide.'

'One breast for the life of the President? I would have

8

to think about it.'

'Maybe you wouldn't have much time to think.'

'Maybe you don't have a gun.'

'Maybe I do.'

'Maybe you wouldn't get close enough to kill her. If you have a gun it has to be small otherwise I'd see it, so it's not like your Lee Harvey with his sniper's rifle or whatever he had. So maybe you're not as big a threat as you think you are.'

'Or maybe I am. Maybe I have military training and know all about close quarter combat. Or maybe that's the chance you have to take. Save the President's life by showing me a breast. It doesn't seem like such a big sacrifice.'

'It's not about the sacrifice.'

'What is it about then?'

'It's about you, a complete stranger, trying to pressure me. For all I know you do this every week, every day. Maybe you've seen every breast in Dublin.'

'For all you know, maybe I have. It doesn't change your predicament. So what's it going to be, are you going to show me your breast?'

'Are you going to show me your gun?'

'That's not how we play this. You have to decide if it's worth the gamble. I may have a gun, I may not. But you definitely have a breast. And it's whether you think it's worth showing it. Knowing that by so doing, there's a chance that you might be saving the President's life.'

'And an equal chance of me being suckered in by a frickin' chancer.'

The doors hissed and the conductor appeared. He said, 'Tickets please,' to the couple three seats back.

Danny Guthrie said, 'If you say anything to him, I'll kill him too.'

9

'If you have a gun.'

'Your call.'

He came to their facing seats and said, 'Tickets.'

She held Danny Guthrie's eyes, and held out her ticket.

Danny Guthrie kept looking at her.

The conductor said, 'Sir?'

Danny Guthrie nodded. But didn't take his eyes off her. He unzipped his jacket enough to remove his wallet from an inside pocket. He slipped out a note without looking at it. The conductor ran off a ticket and handed it to him with the change.

Danny Guthrie said, 'Thank you.'

The conductor moved on. Only when he was gone did Danny Guthrie put the ticket, wallet and change back into his pocket. But this time he opened the jacket a little wider and she thought she saw, she was nearly sure she thought she saw, she was about fifty-fifty sure that she thought she saw the dark outline of something that might or might not have been the butt of a gun.

'So what's it to be?' asked Danny Guthrie.

Two hours later she was naked and exhausted in her boyfriend's bed, in his apartment: first floor, curtains open, the canal beyond. The sun was streaming through the window. She had bruises on her knees from making love on the hardwood floor. She had scrapes on her back from making love against the plumbing in the bathroom. At various points she had shouted, 'Ride me, Napoleon!' and 'Camelot!' in her ecstasy.

The boyfriend was saying, 'You're confusing me. You're quite the tiger, but every twenty minutes you jump up to check the news. Is there something going on I should know about?'

'No, nothing. Just curious.'

He pulled her too him. He kissed her hard. He moved on to her breasts.

She said, 'They're all yours.'

And then in the *mmm* of another kiss, she heard: '*We interrupt this programme for an important news flash. We cross now to ...*'

About the Story

I'VE WRITTEN TWENTY-FIVE books now, and I didn't realise until I was asked to write this short story, that there are virtually no sex scenes in any of them. I was determined to put that right with this story, but, as you will now realise, I didn't. I intended to, but without being unduly wanky about it, the story is what the story is, and I never know what that is until the end. I don't plan in advance. Making it up as I go along is the fun of it for me. I do a lot of my writing at my house in Blanchardstown, on the outskirts of Dublin, but I'm from the north so I'm a frequent traveller on the Dublin Express. Like any writer, my best lines are to be found on the page, not in small talk, so I like to watch and listen, but not partake. I suppose that makes me a bit anti-social. This story is a result then of a question I hear a lot on the train: 'Is anyone sitting here?' My inclination is always to say, yes there is, now bugger off, because you never know what kind of a nut might sit down beside you.

Being a good Northern protestant, I didn't cross the border until I was about twenty years old, and had my first serious girl friend. We would go to Jury's Hotel for naughty weekends. There wasn't much in the way of night life back then, and eating out consisted mostly of going to Captain America's burger bar in Grafton Street, which we considered to be the height of sophistication. For some reason we were also much taken with the prairie dogs in Dublin Zoo. Dublin also had the only McDonalds in Ireland, because they were too frightened, and with good reason, to open on the other side of the border. It felt like going to another country then, and although we're all a lot closer now, it still very definitely feels like another country. But that may be because I don't talk to anyone, you know, in case they're a nutter.

Madeleine. Like Seine
by Shelley Silas

A CREAM-COLOURED TABLECLOTH is covered with six of everything, crystal wine glasses and matching tumblers for water. Tonight the bottled variety will be available, all the way from Tipperary to the bay, sparkling and still. Usually only tap water is on offer.

There are lines of shiny cutlery. An uncut loaf of white bread rests under a square of silk, Hebrew words carefully painted across it. Everything has been set with care and precision.

It is a bit strange, Bernie thinks, to be here, in Dublin with a table set for Shabbat dinner. Strange, because the people who live in this house are not Jewish. Bernie is. They are doing this for him, to make him feel at home. Except in his home he does nothing, he observes nothing. He occasionally eats pork, reserves bacon for weekends. He enjoys the whole process of peeling prawns, dipping his hands in bowls of lemon water, or, if they are not provided, sucking away the detritus from his fingers. And he probably uses his car more on a Saturday than any other day of the week. And, as for women, he has never tasted of his own, never found a girl he wants to take home, show off to his mother. Such is his commitment to being a Jew.

He counts the place settings again, six people, he

knows who three of them are.

Larry Martin, in bare feet, walks softly into the room, chewing gum, more mid-American than middle-class English.

'Relax,' he says, 'help yourself to whatever you want, the others will be here soon.'

Larry Martin, aged sixty-one at his last birthday two months ago, tall and lean, his sandy hair unkempt and bountiful, not a strand of grey showing. He stares out through floor-to-ceiling back doors of glass, stares out at the garden, Bernie's reflection clear and still, behind his own. Larry stares at the copper-coloured mounds that have gathered during the day, swept into corners by a strong easterly wind. Tomorrow he will clear them away, tomorrow he will rake and sweep and make tidy. For now he simply stares at the task ahead, as if willing and hoping that, by magic, come morning his work will be done.

'Er, who are the others?' Bernie asks, wondering if it's rude to want to know who else will be sitting at the dinner table.

'Your flatmates, lodgers, city dwellers,' Larry says, then laughs. 'My wife, the kids.' He corrects himself. 'Hardly kids.'

Bernie counts, five people in total. Five not six.

'Oh, and a friend,' Larry says, 'we thought she'd like you. Now excuse me while I get ready otherwise Madeleine will have a go at me for being late.' Larry pronounces Madeleine so it rhymes with Seine. Bernie repeats it in his head, under his breath, so it will come naturally when he finally meets her. He knows she is ten years younger than Larry, he knows she is attractive, in a way that only red heads can be. She's like Maureen O'Hara, his mother said. But Bernie doesn't know who Maureen O'Hara is.

15

Upstairs the shower pumps away. A radio is switched on, the sound suddenly muted as a door closes on Larry's ablutions. Bernie looks at the table and hears Larry's words again, about the woman, the friend. Larry didn't say "we thought you'd like her," he said "we thought she'd like you".

He hopes Larry has not invested in a round piece of fabric that he will have to place on his head. He hopes they are not expecting him to say the blessing, welcome in the Sabbath. He doesn't know the words, and there isn't enough time to download, print and learn by heart. Since his father died three winters ago, his mother has gone to her sister on Friday nights. Takes a bus there and a cab home, or is offered a lift by one of many invited strangers. His aunt has a reputation for gathering the single, the out-of-towners, the nowhere-else-to-go Jews, who sit at her table for festivals and the Sabbath, who allow her to cook for them and supply endless glasses of wine. Bernie thinks this is her way of recreating a family, for she has none of her own, her husband dead for over fifteen years, the absence of children not so much a part of her conversation these days, though the regret is always there. Bernie is always welcome, but he stays away, leaves the women with strangers, leaves the women to wave their arms in the air and light candles and talk of childhood days, young love and their journey to death and the eventual reunion with their husbands, long gone, buried, their memories continued on a daily basis. The sisters have paid for a bench in a local park, with both their husbands' names inscribed on a narrow brass plaque. To anyone who doesn't know they were brothers-in-law, the significance of two male names means only one thing.

Bernie hasn't had the heart to mention this oversight to his mother or his aunt. They never visit the park any more, and are unaware of homophobic chalk marks against sunburned wood; anti-gay comments about two men who were totally straight.

Bernie is hungry and there is no sign of any food, proper food, chicken or lamb or vegetables steaming or plump dumplings. That's what they have here, he thinks, dumplings. Bernie is starving. Help yourself, Larry said, so Bernie takes a green apple from a bowl on the sideboard, washes it and bites. He has already unpacked, left his clothes on hangers inside a shallow wardrobe, his shoes, two pairs, under his bed. He has looked through the book left on his pillow, stick-it notes of places they think he should visit, Malahide and Dublin Castle, the Irish Jewish Museum, which has a red tick beside it. Bernie has already folded back the edges of his own guidebook, has made a list. He's been here once before, but his interests were different then. He wants to be as much of the city as he can. He will walk and perhaps buy a bicycle, crane and look up at buildings and enjoy his stiff neck, because each second of pain will be a reminder. He will get used to the Euro, find a local pub, make friends, make his house his home. The Liffey will become his river and the Thames a stranger, a tourist he will visit on weekends away. And he will make his students adore him.

Now there is nothing else to do but wait for Larry's family to arrive. He is, after all, in a stranger's house. These are, after all, friends of his parents, not his. Bernie pleaded with his mother not to mention his imminent move to Dublin, because he knew this would happen. He knew he would feel obliged to stay with people he didn't know, in a house that is not walking distance from the places he wants to visit, before the new becomes familiar, before the exciting becomes every day. He told his mother, I'll stay in a hostel, until I can move into my own flat. He even showed her one he thought she would like, sent her a link to their website. The Abraham House Hostel, ten euro a night, with Wi-Fi and an ensuite, right in the city centre. But Bernie Shaw doesn't know how to say no. He never has. It's how he found himself taking a job in Dublin, lecturing to undergraduates on drama and theatre. It's the reason he is in this house with complete strangers, with a table set for dinner, but no dinner to be smelled or seen, no oven switched on, no sign of anything that he would consider a meal.

With his half-bitten apple, he walks around, spit and juice held back with his tongue. The house is a mess, bags of tools in piles everywhere. His mother forgot to mention the building work, but it's too late now. It is dark and he is hungry.

He sees photographs of Larry and Madeleine. And now he knows what Maureen O'Hara looks like, or rather what someone who looks like Maureen O'Hara looks like. She with wavy red hair touching the tips of her shoulders, fair face, a mermaid standing close to the bay. Larry in a white straw hat and dark glasses, his arm tight around his wife, her hand resting on his hip. The sky is idyllic blue, the blue of a child's painting. Bernie smiles at the photos, but he can never understand why people have the need to encase themselves in frames and display them on sideboards and mantelpieces for everyone to see, when the real thing is on offer and so much better. Perhaps, he surmises, the photos are not for their friends but for themselves, to remind them of what was, rather than what is.

Upstairs the pump stops, Larry calls down, 'Won't be long.'

Larry met Bernie at Dublin airport, drove and talked Bernie all the way here. Luckily for Larry, Bernie is a good listener, he knows when to ask questions; in truth he would rather talk about others than himself. Larry made proper coffee and offered him cake, made with apples from the garden, cooked and frozen. Madeleine, he says, is a good baker. They ate and chatted about Bernie's parents then Larry took him to his room. It is debris-free, away from most of the refurbishment, but he must share a bathroom, which he doesn't mind. Only the kitchen-come-dining room is complete.

While Bernie has been walking around, the ground beneath his feet has become warm. He realises it is under-floor heating, rising through his shoes. He slips them off, wriggles his toes. Today he wears a pair of just bought socks, black and silky, he likes the feel on his skin. In a month, or two if he's lucky, holes will appear, for now they are complete. It is six o'clock on a Friday afternoon. Bernie has been in the house for two hours. It feels like two days.

He finds a TV and switches it on. The local news is always so much more interesting when local is other to your own. Different accents, different maps, he finds it amusing. He is just in time for the weather, cold, rain, possible blue skies and more wind. Tomorrow the leaves will have changed direction. This is what Bernie expects. He has packed a selection of clothes, gloves and one scarf, a warm overcoat, his father's overcoat, bought just a week before he died. The rest are layers, which he can add to or take off, depending on the temperature. He is generally a warm man.

Larry emerges dressed and smelling sweet. His cheeks the colour of hot shower blush. He wears black suede shoes and dark grey cords, a white shirt, open at the collar. Bernie notices that Larry's skin, against the brightness of the fabric, is abnormally tanned.

'Everything OK?'

'Yeah,' Bernie says. 'Fine.' And he reaches for his shoes.

'No, you don't need to put them on, really. Be at home. Mine will come off soon enough. Oh,' he says, 'before I forget, is it OK if we use ordinary red wine for the blessing? I remember your father doing it once, when we were over, would that be OK?'

Bernie shrugs, nods. He doesn't mean to nod, it is an automatic response, it's what he always does. 'Great,' Larry says, 'we have some shot glasses, I'll go fill them. I bet you're wondering where we got the cloth from?' Bernie is not wondering about the cloth, he is thinking that if he mumbles quickly no one will understand him anyway, if he talks nonsense, drinks wine and bread, in that order he thinks, wine first and then bread (or is it bread and then wine?) He tries to think back, to when his father was alive; his parents' kitchen, the yellow Formica table, with a leaf at either end. His father sitting at one end, his mother at the other, and Bernie in the middle. Alone. An only child. He can hear his father saying the words, but actions, what about actions? Wine and the bread, he is convinced of this, but he is often wrong, and the pictures won't come.

'We have a Jewish friend, she has a couple of these, her daughter makes them.'

Bernie does not respond.

'Irish Jews, who'd have thought.'

Bernie does not say a word.

'Chaim Herzog was born in Dublin, you know. He founded the Irish Jewish Museum.'

'I know,' Bernie says. He only knows because of the book with the red tick.

'And Leopold Bloom.'

'Yeah, but he wasn't real,' Bernie says.

'You OK?' Larry asks.

'Yeah, fine.'

'Maybe you're tired? Are you tired?'

'No,' Bernie says.

'You can sleep, if you're tired?'

'I'm not tired.'

'Shower? Would you like a shower? Might wake you up.'

'I had a shower.' Bernie reminds him. He has washed and shaved, sprinkled a new perfume he bought at the airport into his pores and rubbed it all over his body.

Larry pulls the cork from a bottle of wine, it eases away smoothly. It is time, he says, to celebrate the weekend. The doorbell rings, Bernie ignores it. It rings again, this time longer. 'Can you get that please,' Larry calls.

Bernie is not used to answering the door in a stranger's house. He is not used to sitting at a table without his shoes, finding interesting subject to discuss with people he doesn't know. Yes, they are kind, yes, they are generous, but he is used to his own company, his own friends' company, people he knows. He has a small but select group of friends, some academics, one from his secondary school, a few from university. He knows what questions to ask them, he knows about their lives, the no-go areas of conversations, the topics they excel at.

He stares at the door and then opens it. His eyes rest on

Madeleine, as she thrusts herself towards Bernie, apologises for not being able to find her keys and kicks off her shoes, talking non-stop. And Bernie is in lust. Bernie is in lust with this Maureen O'Hara look-a-like, dressed in black from head to toe, red hair still red, skin the colour of ripening apricots, eyes the colour of the water in the bay when the sky is watercolour perfect.

'You must be Bernie, hello, I'm Madeleine.' She does not hold out her hand, but moves, instead, to kiss his cheek. He moves his face the wrong way and there, on his lips, her lips, there, on his lips, tender and red, like bleeding cherries. He moves his face away and brushes her skin. It is soft and cold.

'Hi,' he says, 'Yes, I'm Bernie.' He wonders if she can tell that he is becoming hard under his jeans, hard from one look, one kiss. From the smell of her hair, her neck, her face. From the smell of her.

'So pleased to meet you,' she says. 'I've heard a lot about you.' She stands back, takes a good look. 'You look like your father,' she says. 'I should say you look like a young version of your father.' And she smiles and walks away. Madeleine. Like Seine.

A younger version of his father. Is this a good thing, Bernie wonders. What do people say about his father? How do people talk about him? What adjectives do they use? Not tall, he thinks, bald, he remembers. He had hair once. Do they call him handsome? Do they call him sexy?

He follows her all the way to the kitchen, her face lights up when she sees that, in her absence, Larry has at least managed to lay the table, as per her instructions. She kisses him on the lips, holds for a few moments. Bernie can't help but watch. And he is jealous of that moment, that second of husband and wife contact, her lips on his, pressed hard, her lips that were on Bernie's lips. Bernie

22

counts, seven eight nine seconds.

Madeleine is of average height. She is neither fat nor thin, has what Bernie's mother would call a proper woman's body, something men can get their hands on. Now he has the chance to look more closely at her. She wears a black skirt and a fine black cashmere sweater, with three pearl buttons at the top. And she smells divine. Bernie catches himself staring at Madeleine, wondering what is underneath all that fabric, and he starts to walk away, conscious of what is happening underneath his fabric.

'Don't go,' Madeleine says, 'come and talk to us. The others will be here soon. And then we can order.'

It must be Bernie's expression, eyes squeezed together, furrow forming, which makes Larry admit they never cook on a Friday night, they always have a take-away. 'It's what we've always done,' Madeleine says, 'I hope you don't mind.'

Bernie thinks this is funny, amusing to the point of his not believing it. But there is no sign of food anywhere, and now, if he looks at the kitchen again, at the immaculate worktops, free of kitchen debris, except for a bowl of fruit, he can see it resembles a show room rather than a home.

'I thought we'd have a curry tonight, if that's OK.'

'Yeah,' Bernie says, 'I eat everything.' He is looking directly at Madeleine when he says this.

Madeleine looks at Larry. 'Doesn't he look like Ben,' she says.

'Yes,' Larry says, 'He does.'

Stop talking about me in third person, Bernie thinks, and tell me what my father looked like. Description, I need description, I need to know if you thought he was good-looking, passionate. I need to know. And finally there is some hope.

'He was a good-looker,' says Larry.

'Oh yeah,' Madeleine says, 'he was quite a man. Your mother showed us photos, when they were younger. He was quite extraordinary. They were a handsome couple, your parents.'

Madeleine reaches up to a cupboard, and Bernie looks at the line of her arm, encased in soft wool, the tips of her fingers, nails pale pink and pretty. She lets the menu fall to the table, puts a pen beside it.

'I know what I want. What I always want,' she says. 'Bernie?'

He has already decided on what he will have, what he always has. Prawn korma and pilau rice with bindi baji and some poppadoms. Plain not spicy.

'I'm just going to change,' Madeleine says. 'I'll be back in a jiffy.' Jiffy. Rhymes with Liffey. His eyes follow her out of the kitchen, along the corridor towards the stairs. He turns his head just as she turns to walk up, collecting her shoes on the way, heels bashing together in her hands. Larry pours wine. 'I have beer too, if you prefer?'

'Wine is fine,' Bernie says.

They sit and chat about how Larry and Madeleine met Bernie's mother and father, on a Mediterranean cruise ten years ago. It is odd to be discussing an event which Bernie was not part of, a time when his father was still alive. Bernie thinks as people grow older they talk more about their past than the future.

'We were living in London then,' Larry says, 'and we just hit it off, got on, you know.'

'And how long have you been in Dublin?'

'Five years.'

'For work?'

24

'Retirement. Madeleine was born here, but grew up in England. Her heart is here, it always had been. I promised her we would return in our old age.'

'You're not old,' Bernie says.

'You know what I mean. Older. More mature. Me at least. Of an age where we start thinking about different things, where we are in our lives, what we do for the rest of it. And we have a good life here.'

Larry takes an extended mouthful of wine. 'Do you like this stuff?'

'Yeah,' Bernie says, 'It's excellent.' What do I know about wine? he thinks. He usually buys anything on offer, two for one, bin ends, whatever he can afford on his inadequate salary.

Larry looks at his watch. The doorbell rings again, Larry jumps up and walks quickly. From where he is sitting Bernie watches Larry open the door. A woman smiles, and Larry sounds pleased. Larry and the woman kiss each other's cheeks. And while they continue with the niceties, Bernie notices her lean legs are wrapped in almost black. She too wears a black skirt, shorter though, than Madeleine's. He watches her step over the threshold, heels scraping along the floor. She removes her coat and Larry hangs it up, follows the woman who walks towards Bernie.

'Bernie, Fiona, Fiona, Bernie.' Hands held out, they reach and touch. She is not exactly pretty, not exactly unattractive. Her nose is slightly crooked, her brown eyes too close together.

'Hey Bernie,' Fiona says, 'Good to meet you. I hear you're starting at Trinity soon?' She has a different accent to Madeleine.

'Yeah,' he says, 'I am.'

'I've a friend who works there. I can put you in touch

if you like?'

'Sure,' he says.

Larry pours wine for Fiona, goes to phone his children, find out where they are. Fiona and Bernie listen to him, in the hall.

'They've probably been told they have to come,' Fiona says.

'Yeah,' Bernie says, 'and it's probably the last place they want to be.'

'Me too,' Fiona confesses. 'I mean, I like them, Madeleine and Larry, I like them a lot, but they're not my friends, you know. They're not.'

'So why are you here?'

'Because they said someone interesting was coming, and I had nothing better to do and ... I'd better shut up now.'

He likes women who are up-front, women who say it like it is, even if she is only here because it was a choice between Bernie or staying home alone, and she chose him.

'So, Bernie. Are you a Bernard?' She crosses her legs and Bernie crosses his.

'I am. Actually,' he says. 'I am Bernard George.'

'Don't tell me your last name is Shaw?' she says.

'Simon,' he lies.

'Right,' she says, 'because that would have been too much really. Bernard George Shaw, I mean really, don't you think?'

They sip and smile, neither sure what to say next. In the background Larry becomes more angry, more impatient.

'How do you know ...?'

'I work with Madeleine. Or should say for Madeleine.'

Rhymes with Seine.

'She's your boss?'

'Yeah,' Fiona says, 'she's my boss.'

Fiona leans in, moves closer, puts her hand on Bernie's knee and whispers. 'She doesn't need to work, neither of them do. I mean, look at this house.'

He has looked at the house, detached with a large, gravel drive. And he will look again in the morning, when the daylight offers a different view.

'What does she do?'

'Retail.'

'What, a shop?'

'Larry set her up in business, she goes in three days a week. In the city centre. Clothes. Designer, boutique, indie labels, you know.'

Bernie doesn't know. He is not a shopper, buys only when he needs something, when holes appear or shirts have faded to near extinction. He is a cliché and he knows it.

Larry reappears, apology trying but failing to cover his anger.

'Sorry, sorry,' he says, the kids are not coming. I'm really sorry. Shit, Madeleine will be pissed off.' He leaves them alone, goes to break the news to his wife.

'More wine?' Fiona asks.

'Sure.'

She walks into the kitchen like she has walked into it many times before. She is as familiar as he is unfamiliar with these surroundings.

They finish the bottle by the time Larry and Madeleine appear together, solemn-faced, disappointed. Madeleine has changed into a dress, holding her body the way Bernie wants to hold her. Her lips are succulent and juicy and he

27

wants to taste them. And he wants to taste them now. He is not in the mood for curry any more. He wants something more delicious, something that no menu can offer, no two for one deal can supply.

'Look at you two,' says Madeleine.

They are sitting on the same sofa, plush grey suede, soft to touch. They have red lips, red tongues, and Bernie has relaxed into calling her Fi.

'Sorry about the children,' Madeleine says. 'Young people, you know what they're like.'

'Except,' Fiona says, 'they're not that young. And they're our age. My age. And Bernie's age.'

'I'm not,' he begins.

'You're not what?' Madeleine asks.

Bernie shakes his head, dismisses it. He was going to say he's not that young. In relation to Madeleine, he is.

'Let's order,' Madeleine says, and instructs Larry to open another bottle of wine. Except he can't drink any more, because he has to drive. Because the takeaway they like doesn't deliver this far out, even though he is always prepared to pay extra. Because the takeaway is from a restaurant, Madeleine's favourite. Because his wife likes him to go and collect it, she likes to ensure the order is correct, precise, even though Larry will pay for a cab to bring their meal hot and ready and home.

They choose and Larry orders.

'Should we do the ... you know ...' Larry says, pointing at the table, at the bread and shot glasses filled with red wine, 'Before we go for the food?'

'Why not?' Bernie says. For fuck's sake, Bernie thinks, they really want me to do it.

'Oh good,' Fiona says, 'I've never done this before.'

Bernie is loose and relaxed, the wine has made him sparkle. As Madeleine uncrosses her legs he feels his stomach dance. She stands beside him at the table, eager and all ears, ready to receive whatever he gives. Bernie's skin prickles, tingles all over. It is as if someone is kissing his neck and ears and he can't stop it, can't do a thing about it.

Larry covers his head with a napkin, Madeleine just wants to drink the wine. Two extra for her now the kids are not coming. Larry gazes at the kitchen cupboards, Fiona knows she has been set up. She has never had a Jewish man before.

Bernie speaks fast, convincing himself that what he is saying is right. He throws his arms in the air, and passes round the wine. They drink. Madeleine drinks again. And again. He throws his arms some more and cuts the bread. There is no salt, but he doesn't bother to tell them. He is so hungry, he could eat the entire loaf. It isn't the bread he is used to; challah from the shop near his mother's, fresh and soft with a hard crust. This is a white loaf, not sweet enough for his sweet tooth. But it will do.

'Now what?' Fiona says.

'Now we go and get the food,' Larry says.

But tonight it is not Madeleine who will accompany her husband. Tonight the twenty-something Madeleine has spent all day with, the twenty-something who would, she knows, love to sit beside Larry in his silver convertible, listen to his stories and plays classical music, tonight the twenty-something will escort him.

'Just make sure everything's in the order,' Madeleine says as she waves them off, closes the door and returns to her guest.

Bernie is rinsing the shot glasses, tidying the table, trying to distract himself from the woman walking towards him. In the walking, she slips off her shoes, her feet slide along the heated floor.

'How's your mother?' she asks.

Bernie sighs. 'Good, she's good. She said to send you love.'

'Send it back when you speak to her.'

'Of course,' Bernie says, then, 'Yeah, I will.'

He is trying not to catch her accent, mimic it badly, so it will look like he is taking the piss. He is doing anything but taking the piss.

When he turns away from the sink, Madeleine faces the back garden.

'You know, he'll say later on that he'll sweep that up tomorrow. But he won't. He won't.'

'I can do it if you like?'

'I couldn't possibly ask you to do that,' she says. 'You're our guest. And we like to treat our guests properly.'

He wonders if she can feel the earth that is shifting through him. He turns, sits down once more, sips wine.

The house is quiet. So is Bernie.

Madeleine sits at the other end of the sofa. Opposite them a retro clock hangs above the mantle piece. It is seven fifteen. Bernie wonders how long before Larry and Fiona return.

'She fancies him you know.'

Bernie looks up, into Madeleine's cool blue times two.

'Who fancies who?' he asks, unsure he wants an answer.

'Fiona. She fancies him. So I thought, let's see, let's leave them together and see if she tries.'

'Tries what?'

'Oh Bernie, come on, get with it. To seduce him.'

Bernie shakes his head. 'Sorry, who?'

'Larry.'

'Oh,' Bernie says, thinks, says again, 'Oh. He wouldn't?'

'It's not him I'm worried about.'

'How do you know?'

'I know. Trust me.'

'Right. Right.'

The clock ticks, the wind gathers speed, they work their way through the bottle, and gradually, each time she picks up her glass, straightens her skirt which crackles of electricity, Madeleine has inched her way beside Bernie. Right beside Bernie, so he can feel her warmth touching him even though she is not. They say nothing, take it in turn to pour from the bottle, smile, ask inane questions because they have to talk about something. When she puts down her glass he thinks nothing of it. When she stands up, he assumes she is going to open another bottle of wine. When she walks into the kitchen and lifts the phone out of its cradle, he thinks she is calling Larry, to check up on him. Madeleine turns her face away from Bernie, talks softly into the handset. Seconds later she is standing close by, looking down, while he looks up.

'Come on,' she says and takes his hand. He has no idea what come on means, but willingly offers himself, palms sweaty, but so are hers.

'Who did you call?' he asks, as she takes him upstairs, to his single bedroom, with one loose floorboard and a thin shaft of air running in through the window.

'The restaurant. I asked if they left yet. It's twenty minutes away.'

'And?'

'And the person I spoke to said Larry had just paid.'

'So?'

'So if they're not back in twenty minutes, or twenty

31

five, I will know.'

'You will know what?' She throws him down. 'Fuck,' he says.

'I intend to,' she says.

She lays her head on his chest. His heart is beating, 'like a hundred Irish dancers', she says. He finds this funny.

'What's so amusing?'

'Noth–' She kisses him before he can finish the word. She is hard and tender at the same time. She is everything he is not, has never been, would like to be but cannot be. He opens his lips, to speak, her tongue gets in the way of his a, e, i, o. 'You can't,' he says.

'Can't or don't want to?'

'I … I want to.'

'I know. I knew the moment I opened the door. If you really want me to stop me, tell me, get up and walk away.'

But he doesn't. He allows her to explore him, to undo and unbutton, remove the silk from his feet, warm his toes with her mouth. She stays fully dressed in her fitted dress, so easy for him to feel her figure through the material. She knows exactly what she is doing. She's had men younger than this, with firmer skin. But there is something delicious about Bernie. With one hand she undoes his jeans, the button kind. And then her hand is in and under and all over.

He smiles, laughs, he can just about bear this. He lifts his hand, looks at his watch.

'Don't worry,' she says.

And then she is on her back, and despite the wine he is hard and longing for her, this Maureen O'Hara look-a-like, with her red hair and apricot skin, her sweet-smelling neck and stockings. She is wearing stockings. And he is

32

in, just like that. He is in, smooth and easy and he fits. He takes a second, just a second to consider where is he, who he is with, in this single bed in the house where he is a guest, with the woman of the house, while the man buys them dinner. He could take this as a thank you, for making him feel so at home. He really does feel at home. He really does feel welcome.

He is above her and in her and then they swap places and she rides him like a horse at the races. His hands are around her waist, his flesh in her hands, nail digging into him, him pulling her down so he can kiss her. He wants to taste her mouth and teeth and tongue. Her saliva is red wine and mints and something else.

Madeleine, he says. 'Madeleine,' he says,

'Yes?'

'Nothing.'

She laughs and manoeuvres them so that they are sitting up, her back to the wall, Bernie hard inside her, legs bent back, he feels no pain, but later, tomorrow his muscles will ache and he will feel like a real tourist who has explored and found something new.

Bernie inside her, pushing himself into her. Pushing himself against her as far as he can go. He strokes the flesh of her upper thigh, uncovered by black nylon. He is still wearing his shirt, now undone, it tickles her body as he lifts and moves and sways. Her dress is pulled up; stretchy fabric has its uses. The radiator is on and he is boiling hot but right now he doesn't give a damn, about the heat or Larry or his mother or dead father or what he is doing, because right now he wants to be here, in this room fucking this woman because he can. Because he says yes, it's what he does, he says yes without thinking. Only this time he wanted to say yes, he didn't want to think.

She thinks, is this how Mrs Robinson felt?

Outside the wind howls, and Bernie howls and Madeleine grins because she knows she is good. She is the best. She is saving the best for last.

They lie side by side, looking up at the dimly lit ceiling. He turns, licks her face, salt and sweet and expensive tasting. Five minutes to spare before Madeleine hopes she will hear the car pull up, the alarm click twice, the key in the door, the call of *Hello*, the smell of food rising. Bernie tries to sit up, she pushes him back and shakes her head.

'Madeleine, we have to, they'll be, the time.'

'Trust me,' she says.

And he does.

She kisses Bernie, her mouth taking his face and then she draws a line with her tongue from his forehead down between his eyes to his nose above his mouth his lips, and his tongue tries to talk to hers, but she is not in the mood for conversation, down the centre of his neck she pulls open his shirt, down between his shoulder blades, she stops for air, starts again, to his nipples, a circle around each, then a bite to keep him attentive, down to his centre, a good centre, she thinks, muscles taut, muscles hard, down past his ribs, and she waits. And she hovers as he pulls his stomach in because her hair, fallen over her face, is caressing his skin so lightly it is causing him to laugh, but not laugh. It is causing him to pull in his stomach. She listens as a car passes. And keeps passing. He sighs as Madeleine licks and kisses and hovers and looks him in the eyes and smiles. She will have to brush her hair and reapply her lipstick. Then she is down, crushing her head into his pubic bone, holding his hips with her hands and as his body tries to sit up she takes him, takes his cock in her mouth, and he is hard and ready and she thinks he is such a good guest. Probably the best she has ever had. And he looks down and cannot believe what he sees. And he likes it.

'Fuck,' he says. 'Fuck fuck fuck fuck.'

'You can say that again.'

She slips off the bed, drops her dress down over her body. There is not one tear, one snag on her stockings. Impressive, he thinks.

She is out of his room, across the hall, into the bathroom, he hears the water running. He makes his bed, plumps up the pillows, tidies. He opens the window, to remove the smell of sex. His sex and her sex and their sex, carried now quickly across the bay.

She winks at him, as she emerges fresh and smelling sweet, red hair untangled, lips perfect once more. She has checked every inch of material, for a signifier to give away the game. This time she is careful.

Behind a locked door Bernie looks at himself in the mirror, grins incredulously. He grabs the sink, hands on either side, drops his head and softly cries, *Yes*. He is tired, he wants to sleep, but he has to eat and make polite conversation with two people he barely knows. At least Madeleine is not such a stranger any more. He breathes deeply, quenches his hot face.

And then he hears the car pull up, the alarm click twice, the key in the door, the call of 'Hello', the smell of food rising. Madeleine responds with, 'In here.' She has opened more wine, is sitting at the table, her back to the garden, napkin spread across her lap, her appetite wanting something different now. She sips from her lipstick stained glass, is ready to receive Larry and Fiona with serving spoons ready. She can tell her husband has behaved.

'Where's Bernie?' Fiona asks.

'Upstairs.'

'Everything all right?' Larry says, as Bernie enters the room, clean shirt hanging over clean trousers, schoolboy face still flushed and wet. Except his feet are bare. Larry notices and Fiona notices and of course Madeleine notices. Except Bernie doesn't notice, because the floor is warm, the ground is cosy.

'Everything all right? Larry asks.

'Yeah, fine.'

'He had a shower. Didn't you Bernie? To wake him up.'

'Mind if I help myself to a beer?' Bernie says.

'Go head,' Larry says, and he points to a long cupboard, which conceals the fridge.

Bernie sits beside Madeleine and Larry sits beside Fiona.

'Guess what?' Madeleine says. 'Bernie has very kindly offered to clear the leaves tomorrow.'

'Has he?' Larry says.

'I said we couldn't let him, but he insisted.'

'Well,' Larry says, 'that is very kind of you, Bernie.'

'It's the least I could do,' Bernie says, as Madeleine's toes meet his, tickle his feet and then she pulls away.

'As I said before,' Larry says, 'make yourself at home, help yourself to whatever you want. And I mean it. OK?'

Bernie nods. 'OK.'

Under the table hands are meeting, nudging, palms are tickling, fingers are stroking, up and in between. Madeleine drops her hand onto Bernie's cock and he contorts his face. Inside, a sigh so deep, he thinks it's not so bad, staying with my parents' friends after all.

'Food OK?' Larry asks.

'Delicious,' Fiona says.

'Bernie?'

'Excellent,' he says. 'Excellent.'

And in the floor-to-ceiling back doors of glass, Fiona and Larry see it all. The meeting and the nudging and the tickling and the stroking. And the hand on Bernie's cock. But they say nothing. Because it wouldn't be fair.

About the Story

I CHOSE DUBLIN BECAUSE, of the four cities in the anthologies, although I have been there on a couple of long weekends and as a child, it's the city I have spent the least amount of time in, compared to New York, Paris and of course my home town, London. Most people write about what they know, but what I know of Dublin is limited to little more than George Bernard Shaw, the Liffey and Guinness so I thought I would give myself a goal. And of course the story had to be erotic as well. I've never knowingly written an erotic story. Two new challenges for me. But where to start? People, historical landmarks, were there any famous Dublin-born Jews? As I mostly write plays, I chose to write a character called Bernie George Shaw, as a tribute to the great Irish playwright, even though he moved to London aged twenty, and was definitely not Jewish! I then let the play unravel organically. I warmed to Bernie immediately, but I had no idea what he was doing in the city, or in a house with total strangers. I'm always interested in the unknown, so my character could be too. In a way Madeleine is a metaphor for the unfamiliar, as well as the city, she is uncharted territory, new to Bernie, and he explores her in a way he will explore the land. As for location, I didn't want to be in the city centre, but in a more open environment, and I really wanted water other than the Liffey. What better place to set it than a house overlooking Dublin Bay.

Juno and the Peacock
by Severin Rossetti

TEMPLE BAR WAS HIS territory, those cafes and bistros south of the Liffey where he could be found most evenings, preening and posturing, presenting himself as one of God's most splendid creatures. Inches above six foot, with muscles he liked to flex and always a swagger when he entered the company of women, he had to be seen, be noticed, and be admired. The tourists and students, the hen parties and bright young things who flocked to Temple Bar provided him with his audience, his prey.

Juno had been watching him for some weeks now, had studied his manners, knew his habits, and everything about him was an annoyance to her, from the way his elbows splayed out when he stuck his hands in his pockets, strutting about like an arrogant cock, to the habit he had of stroking his index finger across his brow, brushing aside the wayward lock of hair which always found its way back there.

She decided that she would have him. Not as others might have had him, though, for so many had and any woman could; she would not become a part of his stable, another of his conquests. No, she would have him on her own terms.

Petite and slender, Juno would look quite vulnerable

beside him, barely coming up to his shoulder. Insignificant enough to disregard? Or vulnerable enough to tempt him? On such a slender body her breasts appeared quite full, and for the occasion she accentuated them further with a soft lace bra which lifted them and cupped them together invitingly. With the added height he had over her, the low neck of the thin cotton dress she wore would offer him a tempting view. With make-up to suit his tastes rather than hers, a little more obvious than was usual, and a liberal application of perfume, she set out for the bar where she knew she would find him.

He was at the pool table with his mates, posturing as always, a cue resting along his shoulders, behind his neck, and his arms draped over it, hands hanging slackly. She recognised the pose from a James Dean poster, smirked as she wondered if he rehearsed it before the mirror each night. There was certainly a practised easiness about the stance, broadening the back which was turned to her, accentuating the bulging biceps and tapering waist.

She crossed the room, bought a bottle of cold beer, then rested with one elbow on the bar, to wait.

As he circled the pool table it was easy to attract his attention, a smile was all that was needed and she saw his muscles tense, his biceps automatically flex. Looking along the length of his cue at her, his eyes narrowed as he thwacked the balls about the baize, and that swagger she knew so well was back as he sauntered around the table, moving from one shot to the next. The sickly smile he gave her said it all, said *here I am babe, you want me*.

With the bottle of beer to her mouth, her lips just kissing it, she returned his gaze each time he glanced in her direction, as if studying him intently, though she already knew him well enough.

Finally, the game over, he lay down his cue and came

along the bar towards her, his hips rolling, his arms swinging. He clinked his bottle of beer against hers, asked, 'Another one?'

She smiled up at him as she shook her head, tossing her hair back over her shoulder. 'No thanks. I'm fine.'

'Very fine indeed,' he said, in a deep bass drawl which he probably thought was sensual. 'The name's Barry Peacock, but my friends call me Baz.'

'I will call you Peacock,' she said, offering her hand.

'A bit formal. Makes you sound like my employer. Or my teacher.'

'Could be,' she smiled. 'But Peacock suits you, so Peacock you will be. My name is Juno.'

'Juno. Lovely. Luscious lady,' he said, which was rather more poetry than she had expected of him.

Her tiny hand was lost in his and he held it firmly, not quite gently enough, as his eyes travelled down to her cleavage, and there was something unwholesome about the way he regarded her, as if she was being visually molested. She suffered the sensation, though, did not flinch from his grip but kept her eyes fixed on his, matching his direct gaze.

Perhaps she disconcerted him, or maybe he actually was thirsty; whatever the reason, his eyes left hers and he tilted his head back to drain his beer, then set the bottle down hard on the bar. 'That other one now?' he asked, seeing her bottle also empty.

Again she shook her head, said, 'Maybe back at my place?'

To give him credit there was no change in his expression, none of the glee she might have expected of him. But then again, perhaps that was his conceit, that he was so sure of himself. He slipped his big hand around her waist as they moved towards the door, then winked over his shoulder at his pals as if to say *so easy*.

Yes he was! So easy!

Outside, he immediately clutched her to him, crushing her face against his broad chest, his free hand groping her arse, his groin grinding against her. Thankfully it seemed that the height he had over her made him too lazy to bend to kiss her, and patiently she worked her way free of his clumsy embrace. His arm around her shoulder, this she permitted, though tucked into his armpit, as she was, she was aware of his damp perspiration, the slightly stale odour he gave off. But that was alright, he would be sweating even more profusely by the time she had finished with him.

She lived close by Trinity College, in a basement flat whose rooms were low but sprawling, and he had to duck his head to enter as she gestured him in. There was still a hint of the incense she had been burning earlier. Outside in the garden wind chimes tinkled in the light evening breeze, and all around were the objects she treasured, the enamels and the silks, the Buddhas and the dragons.

'It's like entering a sodding temple,' he remarked gruffly, going to sit uninvited on the sofa.

'Where you would worship who? Or what? You do know that Juno was the mother of the gods, don't you?' she prompted; he looked at her blankly. 'I'll go get those drinks.'

She took her time in the kitchen, gave him the opportunity to be bored, restless, inquisitive. When she returned he was looking at the objects on the low table before him, studying each but without much interest. She set the beers down on the floor, waited, then waited a little longer, saw him finally pick up the item she wanted.

'Chinese handcuffs,' she told him, stepping forward.

'Handcuffs? This flimsy little tube?' he said, looking

up and back at her.

'Here, let me show you,' she offered, reaching over him, one arm to either side of him. 'You put your finger in one end, so, the finger of your other hand here. And hey presto! Now pull.'

He tried to pull his hands apart and felt the weave of the thin tube grip his fingers, tugged harder but only succeeded in twisting the tube, not freeing himself.

'Dimwit!' she said, and in an instant had stouter cuffs around his wrists, was yanking his arms up and behind him to fasten them to the back of the sofa.

His head snapped to the left, to the right; while he was still trying to figure out what had happened to him, she was quickly around the sofa and crouching down to shackle his feet to a stout iron bar, spreading his thighs wide apart.

'You really know nothing, do you?' she said, stepping back and regarding him disdainfully, her arms folded. 'All you had to do was push your fingers together and they were out.'

He did as she said and his fingers were freed, but not his wrists.

'Take these fucking things off!' he snarled at her.

'For me to do that you'd have to beg, nicely,' she said, shaking her head, and bent to pick up something else from the table. 'Now, do you know what these are, my pretty little Peacock?'

'Ear rings?' he said, looking at the long black teardrops that she dangled from her fingers.

'Oh my goodness, no!' she laughed out loud, and came towards him, bending close. 'Silly little boy! These are nipple clamps. I've made many a grown man cry with these.'

As Juno brought her face close to his he cursed her and

43

spat in it. Slowly she wiped the spittle from her cheek, smeared it across his and then slapped him hard, first with the flat of her hand, then with a backward swipe.

'You bitch! I'll fuck you in two for that!' he threatened.

'No you won't, little man,' she said, bending once more, hooking fingers in his shirt and ripping it open. She twisted a bared nipple viciously between finger and thumb, then fixed one of the clamps on it, drawing a sharp intake of breath from him. 'Brave little boy,' she smiled, closing the second clamp a little more savagely on his other nipple.

While his eyes were closed to fight the pain she unfastened his jeans and tugged them down to his knees, then his shorts too. Trailing her fingers along the underside of his raised arm, she felt him flinch as she walked around the sofa to stand behind him once more.

'Ticklish too?' she whispered, resting her cheek against his, letting her fingers run over his shoulders and down his chest. 'Well there will be nothing as nice as ticklish for you. For you I'm afraid that it has to be pain.'

She flicked the clamps to set them swinging, tugging at his nipples, then scratched her long nails over the swollen buds. And as his nipples reddened, as their pain grew, she began to lick at his ear.

'You see, vain macho men need to learn their position with respect to women. And at the moment yours would seem to be pretty pathetic, wouldn't you say? Though to my mind much more preferable to the arrogant posture you've adopted in the past.' She set the clamps swinging harder, bringing an audible sigh from him now, said, 'That is something we must remedy, something I will cure you of.'

A hiss escaped his lips, it might have been a curse

disguised but she preferred to think not, asked, 'Does it hurt? Is there pain now?'

His eyes were closed, his head was bowed, his jaws were clenched.

'Well?' she demanded, plucking at one of the clamps.

'Yes!' he cried.

'Then why does it excite you?' she asked, softly now. 'And you can't deny that it does. I can see that you're excited. So tell me, Peacock, why *does* the pain excite you?'

There might have been a whimper now, but no coherent reply. She walked around the sofa, her fingers running through his hair, down his face, and knelt between his spread thighs. She looked at his erect cock, brought her face closer to it as if for a better look, then licked her tongue just once across its tip.

'Oh look how it dances for me!' she exclaimed, as his penis sprang up at her touch. 'The proud little cock is dancing for Juno, and her a mere slip of a girl while he is such a macho man! How does it feel to be under her control?'

'Suck it bitch,' he said, but there was no force in the words, he was weakening.

'Later perhaps, if you're a good little boy, if you beg,' she smiled, and taking his cock in her hand, began to stroke it slowly. 'And you *will* beg, I promise you, beg for me to give you the pleasure which will make all this pain worthwhile.'

She stroked his cock for a while, then brought up her hand to show him another of the teardrop shaped clamps.

'No nipples left, so where can I put this one?' she wondered quizzically, and slipped her hand beneath his balls, stroked her fingertips across them, then took a pinch of skin between finger and thumb, plucking at the sack.

She paused a moment to look up, to see the fear in his eyes.

'No!' he said, guessing her intentions.

'Yes,' she insisted, and slowly allowed the clamp to close on the fold of skin, then let it go so that its weight pulled his balls down.

Though he cried out, his cock got even harder; though there were now tears in his eyes they were also bright with excitement. Juno rose on her knees to kiss a tear from his cheek, licked her tongue across his lips, nibbled at his ear.

His breath was coming in short heavy pants now, when she placed her hand on his chest she could feel his heart racing.

'You want to come.' She knew. 'Be a man, swallow your pride, be honest and admit it. You ache for the pleasure I can give you.'

When he made no answer she lifted the clamps which hung from his nipples, looking at him sternly, raised them to take their weight and ease the pain for a moment. Before he could smile with the relief, though, she began to pull on them.

'Don't you, Peacock?' she demanded.

'Yes! Yes!' he screamed.

'Yes, what?' she smiled sweetly, making circular motions with her hands, tugging his nipples around and around.

'Make me come!'

Not let him go, or take the clamps off. No. Make him come.

'Then now is when you start begging, nicely,' she said, letting the clamps fall heavily, bringing a cry from him which was quickly replaced by a sob of delight as she grasped his cock again, taking it in both hands and rolling

46

it between them. 'You will say please, you will be respectful in your request, you will call me Mistress as you entreat me. Do it now!'

'Please! I beg you! Make me come!'

Juno's hands slowed, barely moving against his cock, as she prompted him. 'What do you call me as you entreat me?'

'Mistress! I'm begging you Mistress! I need to come!'

'Good boy,' she congratulated him, one hand now beginning to stroke his cock slowly again, her other closing around his balls to apply a gentle pressure. 'Of course you need to come. You need your Mistress, don't you Peacock?'

'I do!'

With each upward stroke her thumb would rub over the head of his cock, smearing the juices about the wet tip; with each downward stroke she would bring his balls up to meet her hand, pressing them into the root of his cock.

'You belong to me now. You know that, don't you?'

'Yes Mistress!' he sobbed. 'I belong to you!'

'Good,' she said, pumping his cock faster, tightening her grip on his balls. 'And now that that has been agreed ...'

'Yes!' He let out a cry as strong as any the pain had brought from him, feeling his orgasm build, feeling her hand squeezing, coaxing it. 'Yes!'

'No!' Juno laughed, pulling her hands away 'No!'

'Huh?'

'Poor little Peacock. What you need is an audience! It's what your vanity thrives on!'

There was laughter from behind him as a second woman came from the kitchen and stepped around the sofa. She was of a similar build; short, slight, with full breasts. They might have been sisters, but Juno introduced her as her friend, her flat-mate, Lucina.

'Pleased to meet you, Peacock,' Lucina smiled, quite affably, as if his predicament was nothing out of the ordinary. They might just have met in a bar, or at a party.

Had they? he wondered, as the two women embraced and sat one to either side of him on the sofa. There was something familiar about the woman. But then he had known so many.

'Now if you were an educated man, Peacock, rather than the macho brute you are, you might know that Lucina is an epithet for Juno, another manifestation so to speak.'

'My name means "she who brings children into light",' Lucina explained.

'You did remark that I sounded rather like a teacher, when I said I would call you Peacock,' Juno reminded him, settling her body closely against his, then looking across him to her friend. 'So, Lucina, what do we do with vain men who get erect so easily, without permission?' she asked.

'Torture their cocks so they learn not to?' Lucina smiled.

'It's the fittest punishment,' Juno agreed, resting her hand on his bare thigh and looking down with disdain at his naked groin. 'But poor little Peacock has grown limp already!' she observed.

'Then we must make his cock hard again before we punish it,' said Lucina, her hand moving to his other thigh.

Both hands began to creep slowly upwards and he tried to squeeze his knees together, hiding his genitals.

'Tut Peacock!' Juno chided him. 'I should slap you for that, but ...' She took his limp prick in her free hand and shook it, let it flop from side to side. 'Sorry little thing,' she said. 'Like a worm, hanging from the worm that he is.'

'Pale and lifeless, like an overcooked piece of pasta,' Lucina said, and they laughed.

'As Molly Malone might have said ... cock-less and muscles!'

'Alive alive-o!'

Juno squeezed his cock gently, but there was little response; she dug her sharply manicured nails into it, scratched up to the head and then released it.

'Dirty little wanker has wanked himself empty, has he?' she frowned. 'What might bring the life back to his sorry little dick? What might make his spunk rise again?'

'Our mouths?' Lucina wondered.

'Our tongues on his balls?' Juno suggested, and smiled cruelly at him. 'You'd better get hard for us, Peacock, or it won't just be your cock we punish.'

The warning given, the women bowed their heads over his groin, Lucina scratching his thigh when she felt him tense. Slowly Juno ran her lips up and down his cock, her tongue flat against it like a cat licking at cream, while Lucina put her lips to his balls and began to nip at his scrotum.

He feared becoming erect, feared the consequences, sweat broke out on his brow but he was unable to resist the ministrations of the two women, especially when they brought their hands into play. Fingers ran up and down his cock, teasing, then linking around it, Juno and Lucina gripping it as if to say it was theirs.

Which of course it was. He – and it – now belonged to them.

Slowly it stiffened, thickened, lengthened, and he let out a sob of despair when Lucina cupped his balls and squeezed, when Juno took his cock between finger and thumb and flicked her tongue quickly across the tip.

'A response at last!' Juno smiled. 'You were never going to be able to resist, were you Peacock?'

She and Lucina raised their heads in unison, keeping their hands on his genitals as they nestled their bodies close into him, Juno kissing him lightly on the cheek as if with fondness.

The gesture made him tremble with trepidation, for such a mocking travesty of affection could only hint at one thing, that there was something other than affection to follow.

'But it seems to be getting dark,' Juno remarked, looking about the room. 'I think candles are needed, so that we can see what we're doing.'

'And so Peacock can see!' Lucina added, with a wicked laugh, giving his balls a gentle squeeze and then rising to leave the room.

'Now keep hard for us dear,' Juno coaxed, her fingers still running up and down his cock, her thumb brushing across its tip from time to time. 'Stay hard for Juno, yes?'

'Yes, Juno,' he was forced to say, knowing it was inevitable that he would stay hard in her hands.

Lucina returned with candles which she lit and placed at intervals around the room, came to the sofa with the last two and sat back down beside him. Holding one of the candles before his face, she kept it steady while Juno reached over to light it, then moved it slowly before him so that the flame danced in his eyes, reflecting his fear. For minutes the three of them regarded the candle in silence, Juno's fingers still caressing his cock to keep him hard.

Then her hand was still, she bent his stiff cock painfully forward and held it delicately by the tip. Lucina inclined the candle a little, first one way and then the other, regarding it as if with curiosity. Molten wax began to spill down the side, she tipped it further as she positioned her hand over his groin.

Both women laughed as Peacock screamed, the hot wax splashing along the thick shaft of his cock. So fierce was his reaction that it sprang from Juno's fingers and she tutted.

'I think I need to hold it more firmly,' she said, waiting for the wax to cool and harden and then wrapped her hand around his cock so that only the head protruded from her fist.

'No!' he begged, and tried to avert his gaze, but hands kept his head bowed, so that he could see Lucina begin to tilt the candle once again.

A single drop of wax spilled onto the tip of his cock, sealing the narrow slit, and he screamed in agony, then again as more fell. He was writhing in their embrace by the time the head of his cock was completely covered, and while the wax was still soft Juno pressed her thumb lightly on the tip, leaving her print like a brand.

'There,' she said, letting his cock fall free. 'That should stop the little wanker coming until we say he can.'

'Yes, it's going to take an ejaculation of some power to burst through that wax seal!' laughed Lucina, blowing smoke into his face as she extinguished the candle.

'Could Peacock build up to such an orgasm?' Juno wondered, stroking his cock steadily, pleased to see that the wax was pliable enough not to break. 'Or will he perhaps never be able to come again?'

As she caressed his cock so Juno kissed his face, first to taste his tears and then for her amusement, whispering obscenities in his ear to coax him to become ever harder in her hand. Lucina, meanwhile, had set aside the extinguished candle and taken up a new one. Now she whittled away at the blunt end with a sharp knife, humming softly to herself, occasionally pricking him with the needle-sharp point of the blade, touching it to his thighs, his belly, the soft undersides of his raised arms.

'Should we put him to the test?' she wondered, when she had the base of the candle tapered to a point. 'See if he is able to come?'

'Indeed, let's!' agreed Juno, and they stood, ordering him to do the same.

With his hands fastened behind his head, and his legs spread by the iron bar, he found this difficult, struggling to rise from the sofa, and they laughed at his clumsiness, prodded him and slapped him and told him to get up. Finally, in what was as close to pity as they could ever feel for him, they each hooked a hand through his arms and hauled him to his feet.

Juno then lay back along the length of the sofa and lifted her skirt to bare her naked thighs and belly.

'Come taste me, eat me, drink me Peacock,' she invited, her body gently undulating.

Lucina helped Peacock lower himself between Juno's thighs, settled him with his face on her friend's cunt, and then the skirt fell over him like a silken shroud, bringing darkness to his world.

Immediately his mouth began to work on Juno's cunt, he kissed, he licked, he forced his tongue inside her. It was an automatic reaction, as if he had been programmed, as if he had been trained.

Lost within the folds of her skirt, between her thighs, he was aware of nothing but her cunt until he felt something press against his anus. Slowly Lucina forced in the whittled end of the candle, twisted it around, pressed it deep.

'Lift your arse a little higher Peacock,' she said, her

hand moving the candle like a joystick to show him the way, and his knees shifted up the sofa, his buttocks raised. 'There's a good boy!' she said, stroking the backs of his thighs, fingertips lightly touching his balls.

He could hear little, and certainly not the striking of the match; he continued to lick and suck at Juno with a delighted devotion. It was only when the first drop of hot wax fell on the back of his thigh that he stopped, when the second and third fell that he cried into Juno's cunt. He tried to pull his head away but she had him clamped between her thighs, all he could move was the lower part of his body, which began to writhe. The angle of the candle then changed, the next drops of wax fell onto his balls and now he screamed.

At last the wax stopped falling, he trembled and waited but there was no further stinging pain and he sighed his relief, his soft exhalation warming Juno's cunt.

Over the tent of her skirt, beneath which Peacock continued to work with his mouth, Juno smiled, seeing Lucina tilt the candle to a sharper angle. Now the wax no longer dripped from it, but poured steadily down its length, accumulating, moving lower, until finally …

His scream was muffled by Juno's thighs and the folds of her skirt, but she felt it shake her cunt as the wax poured onto his anus. A molten pool formed around the base of the candle, spilled across his arse, and before it could harden Lucina removed the candle and upended it, pouring a constant stream of molten wax over the puckered hole.

'That's two orifices plugged!' she giggled, bending down to blow across his arse, helping the wax to cool and harden. 'So which next my love?' she asked Juno.

'I don't think Peacock heard that,' said Juno, and lifted her skirt, parting her legs to let him remove his face from her groin.

Taking him by his cuffed hands, Lucina roughly jerked him away and to his feet. 'What I said, Peacock, is that we now have two orifices plugged.'

'And what we wonder,' added Juno, standing beside him, 'is which we should deal with next.'

'A hood would be good,' said Lucina, running her fingers over his face. 'A tight leather hood which would plug everything.'

'But you know how our words can torment and tease him,' said Juno, licking at his ear, biting at the lobe. 'He needs to hear at least.'

'But not to see. The worm isn't worthy enough to set eyes on us,' said Lucina, and in an instant was behind him, binding a soft leather mask across his eyes.

'And his sobbing and bleating is beginning to annoy me,' Juno decided, so she bound a similar length of leather across his mouth.

There were moments of silence then, the only sound Peacock's heavy breaths as his chest heaved. Seeing nothing, teetering on legs which were spread wide by the iron bar, his body began to sway unsteadily, so the two women pressed against him, sandwiching him between their bodies.

'The only thing you have to excite yourself now, Peacock, is what you feel,' Lucina told him, her hands caressing his body, front and back.

'And what you hear,' Juno whispered. 'Will it be enough to make you come? Come hard enough to shoot that plug of wax from your cock?'

Lucina laughed. 'If not, young man, if you stay plugged, you'll be full of shit and piss and spunk by the morning!'

He shivered at their touch, trembled at their words,

shuddered between them.

'You are frightened, Peacock?' asked Juno, and scratched her nails across his chest. 'Ah! Poor thing!'

'The only thing you have to fear is the silence,' Lucina told him, her lips brushing his ear as she spoke. 'The silence ... and the anticipation of what is to come next.'

And there was a silence so deep that he cried behind his blindfold, sobbed behind his gag. A silence so profound that Juno and Lucina seemed to grow with it and took on the stature of goddesses.

In the presence of such goddesses even the proudest of men could be made as meek as the most insignificant of creatures.

FLYING FROM LIVERPOOL TO Dublin is like being shot out of a cannon; no sooner do you reach cruising altitude than you're plummeting back to earth again. Not the most pleasant of flights, despite (or because of?) the usual company of priests and nuns leafing through their prayer books or fingering their rosaries, but worth it, for Dublin is the place to go for a drink. The chat and the banter; the music and the good humour; the *craic*. I found it in plenty, in places too countless to mention. But then, in Temple Bar …

Peacock *does* exist, though perhaps it is not necessary to go to Dublin to find him. He frequents bars rather than pubs, drinks bottled beer rather than draught, has good looks and charm and is all too aware of the fact. Some men might react violently to his vanity, that is in the nature of the male, but women have subtler ways.

I was brought up in an Irish community in England and remember the matriarchs, the women who could quell us unruly kids with the flick of a finger or a single withering glance. Their husbands might have thought themselves the head of the family, their sons might have towered head and shoulders above them while still in their teens, but it was the women who ruled: the mothers and the grandmothers. Despite their slight stature it was they who had the force, the drive, the determination.

And Juno, I remember her too. Or, rather, I remember Sean O'Casey's play, *Juno and the Paycock*. I have never read it, or seen it performed, but the title has always been enough to intrigue me. An

Irishwoman named Juno? Who was she? Was that a common name? And the *Paycock*? These were questions enough to keep me interested, and from time to time I would imagine my own scenarios, my own plots, to go with the title. *Juno and the Peacock* represents my latest imagining, and the first to be put down in print. Now I think I might see how Sean O'Casey imagined it.

Love is the Drug
by Ken Bruen

I'M GONNA FESS UP, up front.

Kay?

I came to Dublin to fall in love.

Twenty-nine years old, not bad-looking, a girl once told me I looked like the drummer in Bon Jovi.

Yanking my chain, right.

But I rolled with it and sheet, I even considered taking lessons, on the drums that is, not the girl.

My mom was from Dublin so you can already see where I'm coming from.

Cockles and Mussels

Sweet Molly Malone

Trinity College

Real pints of the black stuff and

Best of freaking all

Phil Lynott's home town.

Man, I love that band.

Have the T-shirt and all their albums, not on CD, nope, on vinyl.

Serious bucks that.

My old man, worked construction in Jersey so guess what?

I work construction.

I do the edgy stuff, out on the high beams, and it pays.

Mega.

Did me a shit load of overtime for me dream trip.

Two weeks in a hotel in Temple Bar as the internet said it was the centre of the action.

Gonna get me an Irish girl, got to be at the core.

I had close to ten K to spend in that 2 weeks. And I was excited.

My dad had passed away a few years before and I was still living with my mom, she kept giving me advice:

1............Don't let them take you for an ejit.

2..............Mind yer money.

3...................Be sure and eat a good breakfast.

4.......................Don't be having sex with foreign ones!

I guess No 1 and No 4 are kinda interchangeable.

She gave me rosary beads, to keep me safe and a bottle of Holy Water.

Homeland Security took the Holy Water.

I flew Aer Lingus, gonna make it Irish all the way.

I was in economy, keep the green for the coleen. I had an Irish Claddagh ring, heart turned outwards to show I was available.

An elderly man in the seat beside me, sipping from a flask.

I put out my hand, said

'I'm Ted, Ted Newton, outta Jersey.'

He chugged on that flask, like Mother's milk, ignored my hand, said

'Let me guess, first trip to Ireland.'

It showed?

I said

'Yes.'

He made what sounded like a snicker, said

'They'll see you coming.'

I didn't want to ask what that meant as I figured, good it wasn't.

So I put on my iPod and heard him say

'Fookin Pogues I'll bet.'

He was right but I acted like I hadn't heard him.

When the drinks trolley came, I had me a double Jameson and I would have offered him a drink, my treat but he'd already asked for a large brandy, ignoring me completely.

The in-flight movie was a Ben Stiller gig so I skipped that, moved my tracks to *The Boys are back In Town.*

My companion was snoring loudly by then and I was a relieved.

Not that I'm a wuss.

You fucking kidding me, guy?

I'd been working construction since I was eighteen years old and I was built.

You don't survive the job for eleven years by eating shit sandwiches but my first real Irish person, I didn't want to break his goddamn nose right off.

The in-flight meal was curry

On an Irish airline ? But there was some seriously good bread, I asked the hostess who was as hostile as my sleeping buddy, I asked

'Is that like, like, real Irish soda bread?'

She said, yah believe it,

'Whatever?'

I had an Irish coffee for afters, determined to keep up my Irish dream. It tasted like the crap they peddle in Coney Island with fake cream on it and the hostess said

'That will be ten Euro.'

She accepted 15 bucks with a sigh.

I could have argued the rate of exchange but the sooner I got off that goddamn airplane …

Irish Immigration busted me balls, every which way but loose.

I was losing the Irish buzz.

Finally, after I changed me dollars to Euros and was staggered at the rate, not in my favour, I got outside and you guessed it, it was raining.

I'd grown up with the lilt of soft Irish rain.

This was mean, vicious, New York kind of shit.

Finally got a cab, the driver was Polish and smoking.

I pointed out the no smoking decals all over his vehicle and he muttered

'Is no Iraq here.'

The fuck was that.

I gave him a tip and did he thank me?

Right.

Temple Bar looked like fucking Scranton, the armpit of Jersey.

The hotel.

I don't want to sound like one of those moaning, ever-whining Yanks but shitsville USA, here it was in Dublin.

And two weeks in this dump.

Jesus H. Christ.

I threw my backpack on the unmade bed and headed out.

Get a pint.

That was the Irish way.

So my *Lonely Planet Guide* said.

Found my way to a pub called Mulligan's, supposedly where James Joyce drank.

A Ukrainian barman.

By now, I was so freaked out, I almost didn't give a flying fuck.

The taps of
Bud Light

Coors

Miller

Weren't helping.

I ordered a pint of Guinness.

I'd heard the real pint took about five minutes to pour, let the head settle, build up to a real sense of Ireland.

Nope.

He poured it straight and pushed it over, said

'Eight Euro.'

I asked him for a wee Jameson, trying to still retain my dream and he said

'We?'

I said

'Whatever.'

Seemed to be the national response.

I was sitting with my miserable ruined pint, the dregs of a bottle of Jameson in a dirty glass and feeling as crushed as The Yankees when Rodriguez blew it on the last innings.

Half thinking to cut me losses and just cash in my ticket, get the fuck outta Dodge.

Heard

'Can't be that bad?'

Looked up to see a vision of bliss.

A girl in her twenties, dressed in jeans and a tight-fitting black T-shirt, auburn hair to her shoulders and oh Thank you Jesus, a real Irish accent.

I said

'Not a great day.'

She sat on the stool opposite, said

'You're American.'

I asked

'It shows?'

She laughed, gorgeous teeth, to match her gorgeous

blue eyes.

I'm a Jersey guy, sorry but I thought

'Hooker.'

Why else was she talking to a loser like me.

She said

'Let me guess, your first day, you're probably staying in Temple Bar, the seventh circle of hell and the famous Ireland of the thousand welcomes isn't exactly in evidence?'

She'd been reading me mail.

I said

'Exactly.'

I was already in love with her brogue, that soft lilt, almost like a song. She said

'And you're thinking … I'll go home.'

Before I could answer, she put out her hand, said

'I'm Catherine, you can call me Cathy.'

Like there'd be a future?

I wiped my hand on my damp jeans, took her hand, said

'Ted, Ted Newton, outta Jersey.'

She gave a wonderful laugh, said

'Ted, way too much info, rein it in.'

And that's how it started.

She showed me the real Dublin

The Liberties

The old Quays

Where Lizzie had their first gig

Stephen's Green, the back part where U2 had released the sheep when they were made freemen of the city

Three whirlwind days of bliss.

The third night, she came back to my hotel, the bed had been made (by me) and we made slow lingering love despite the crescendo of noise from Temple Bar in full

63

roar.

Jesus, I was in love.

The dream was not only possible, it was happening.

She was a great listener, seemed interested in all me stories of construction and Jersey, even asked me if I'd ever seen Bruce.

I had.

One time on the Jersey shore, walking his kids, he'd nodded hello and she was impressed, asked

'What's he like?'

I said

'A working stiff, you know, blue-collar.'

I wanted to riff on Thin Lizzie, but if she liked Springsteen, ok.

Asked me my favourite song of his, I said, even though Tom Waits wrote it,

'Jersey Girl.'

She gave a deep sigh, and we made love all over again.

She was it.

The reason I'd worked all those hours out on the ledge, the high winds blowing like banshees, the money I'd saved.

I'd found her.

She was Irish

Seriously gorgeous

And

Appeared to be into me.

So I proposed.

Nuts … right?

She seemed shy then asked

'Will it mean I get a green card?'

Hello?

Duh.

I said

'Am, I guess so.'

She was up on her elbow, we'd made love twice in one afternoon, with room service to act as pit stops, and she never looked so beautiful, she asked, in a more serious tone,

'You're not sure?'

I was mellow, the afterglow of the love making, her beside me, the room service of BLT's and Hot Toddies had made me beyond chilled, I said

'What's it matter?'

Her face changed, she nigh spat

'I get a green card or not, I mean I fucking marry you, I get a green card, don't I?'

It got a little heated after that.

I won't go into the details as they are ugly as I was hoping to tell this as a love story.

But …

… Wait

All was not lost.

We agreed to meet beside the statue of Phil Lynott the next day, I'd have bought the engagement ring and ensured she'd get a green card.

I'd ring the embassy, check it out.

Next morning, I woke late

My wallet was gone.

And my mom's Claddagh ring, I'd left on the bureau, gone.

That was a time ago.

I went into freefall for I don't know, some weeks I guess.

The money ran out and the hotel, they ran me out.

Most days, I stand beside Phil's statue, ask for handouts, foreigners are especially kind.

Go figure.

There's a busker down the street a bit, he only ever plays

'Love is the drug'

I was never really a Roxy Music fan but you know, it kinda grows on you.

My wild Irish yearning has faded.

I don't mind.

Too much.

I know Catherine will show, she just got delayed.

And I have a green card.

It says

Joe's Pizza, take-away, 24 hours a day.

And call it intuition but, I kinda know, Joe will keep his word.

Sounds like a blue-collar type of guy.

About the Story

I WROTE THE STORY by trying to channel Maxim. I asked myself, if Maxim were American, came to Ireland and is the lapsed romantic I've always suspected, what would he write?

And that's the genesis of the story.

All apologies to Maxim for transforming him into the poor soul depicted here.

Maxim of course is nothing like the character and the sadness is of course, purely fictitious ... well, mostly!

Picking Apples in Hell
by Nikki Magennis

'Romantic Ireland's dead and gone'
– William Butler Yeats

IT WAS NEARING DUSK. Students, socialites and Europeans gathered below a broody August sky, drinking wine and staying very carefully blasé about each other. I blended right in. Frank didn't. Yes, he may have been a native son, but after so many years something had changed. I couldn't work out if it was him or Dublin.

'So what's dragged you back, Frank.'

'Oh, c'mon now. Can't a man visit his home town without good reason?'

'Don't try telling me you were missing the ole place,' I said, keeping my voice nice and flat.

What I didn't say was: *'tell me you were missing me, tell me you couldn't forget me, tell me you'd cross the sea just for one more shot of that filthy, mind-blowing fucking we used to do.'*

Frank looked around the plaza. He shrugged. The leather of his jacket was so worn it didn't even make the ghost of a creak. Lines were folded deep into the hide, like the crow's feet at the corner of his eyes. Oh, there was a glimmer of the same old Frank. Eyes as black as ale and as potent. Skin the colour of rain-washed bronze.

'I can hardly recognise the place,' he said, shaking his head kind of sorrowfully. 'It's just as full of shiny shite and fecking foreigners as any other city.'

We were sitting out in Meeting House Square, watching a film they were playing on the wall. I couldn't tell you what it was, other than it had subtitles and real sex in it and took itself deadly serious. I was trying to show Frankie how different it all was now, how I'd changed and the city had changed and how I was no longer the kind of woman ye'd fumble with in the back of some spit and sawdust ole pub. How we were sophisticated, you know, and avoided talk of politics and religion and all those embarrassments.

'Christ, would you look at the state of that,' Frank said.

Beside the art gallery, a gaggle of Liverpool girls screeched. One of them was throwing up in the corner. They'd matching pink cowboy hats with fluffy trim, and bras over their T-shirts, and they were shedding glitter in cascades.

Inevitably, it attracted the attention of a handful of local lads, who stood and catcalled oblivious to those of us pretending to watch the movie. A chorus of tutting tourists couldn't put a dampener on the boys' spirits, and the to and fro of young lust continued as bawdy and desperate as ever.

'Sure some things never change, eh?' Frank said, smirking. I wondered if he was looking at my haircut, the exact copy of that I'd seen on Cate Blanchett, only not as blonde on account of my scalp trouble; my shoes that were knock-off Louboutins from eBay and only a little scuffed around the heel, and the red shift dress I'd put on to look casually thrown together, after changing, of course, forty or fifty times over in the effort to hit on the look that would show just the perfectly right mix of indifference and old-fashioned allure to ensure a night that satisfied not only my loins but my tender, hopeful ego, too.

I expect it was mostly lost on Frank. He was more of a split-crotch panties man, after all. I watched him checking my tits to see if they were still there. He chewed his lower lip. His knee was jiggling twenty to the dozen, and I didn't miss a furtive glimpse at his watch.

I tossed my hair.

'You'd be surprised, Frank. Some of us are different people now.'

'S'that right? Well, yer eyes are still as blue as the sea, Niamh.' He leaned in close. 'And I'll bet your sweet cunt's still as wet between your legs.'

I'd have kissed him or slapped him, no doubt, had the crowd of young lads not distracted us at that moment, shouting out sing-song taunts at the cinema ushers, playful like, but with that ragged edge that meant anything could go pear-shaped at any moment.

Friday night in Temple Bar. Oh, it was dressed up with fresh paint and flower boxes in the windows and the bartenders may polish the fecking cobblestones daily, but when the night drifted in from the docks and the beers started to flow there was little you could do about the panhandlers and the prostitutes and the skangers loitering with intent and the overall tide of floating human flotsam that wash up in a city looking for the craic, and possibly crack if not absolute gallons of strong drink, and, at last at the end of the night, looking most intently for the solace of a nice warm crack to sink their dirty flutes into – whether it belonged to man, woman or something in-between.

A couple of Garda rocked up and tried to skirt around the fracas without actually getting overly involved, and

Frank decided it was time to retire somewhere with a better view, that is, somewhere he could smoke one of his foul European cigarettes without being coughed at.

'Come and see where I'm stayin',' he said, and I smiled.

'Somewhere nice?' I said. Him an international traveller now, I'd visions of room service perhaps and clean sheets. He'd try it on, of course, expect to have me on my back within ten minutes. No doubt I'd be happy to oblige.

We walked down towards Trinity, skirting buskers and drunks, the backs of our hands grazing occasionally, casual, like. Even that was enough to make my heart beat like a pattering clock, and the fact of us, Niamh and Frank, walking together again through the old haunts. Those streets, they were layered up with so many half-remembered stories they were like fly posters pasted over one another, dissolving pictures I caught out the corner of my eye.

How fine we looked back then. Me with my Madonna-bleached hair and his leathers brand new and shiny. Our legs scissored alongside each other's in perfect time, when we were running from Grafton Street up towards the Green. We always seemed to be running.

I could hear echoes, too.

Us laughing, spraying the sound all over the cobbles like frothing beer. The thrum of his old scooter's engine, the fury in his voice. The high breaking note in mine as I shouted after him. All the anger that rained down around us.

I can hear, still, the silence the day after he left. The long, endless grey hush of it drifting in from the quay – *The air so soft that it smudges the words.*

'Brings back memories, eh?' Frank says, and he was

smiling into the breeze like he knew exactly what I was thinking. Cocky shite. Always had been. But I'd always fallen for it, likewise. As he grabbed my wrist and pulled me out the way of a stray skateboard outside the Central Bank, I got that roaring all over, the itch and the hunger for him. To be enfolded in him. Jarred by him. To scrape against the rough of his cheek and to fire up the blue in his eyes and to taste the diesel, the cigarettes, the other women on his fingertips.

We pushed through a crowd of miserable-looking black-haired, black-eyed teenagers and I glimpsed them turn to look after Frank. He'd trouble written all over him, you see. Irresistible to the young and foolish. And part of me must have still been those things, buried under my well-educated, socially mobile, culturally aware self. Yes, part of me was still the culchie, redneck girl from the bogs of Galway, entranced by the street lights, by Frank, by everything in the great, dear, dirty city. Blushing despite myself as he ran one finger over the pale skin on the inside of my wrist. Reading my skin like Braille.

There was a cluster of buskers planted on every corner and we were serenaded along the streets by fiddles, bodhrans, an out of tune guitar and a chorus of straining, echoing voices, the rough edges of them chafing my ears. Frank's hands slid around my waist. I only pulled away for a moment before I gave in and let his hip bump against mine. It felt good.

We passed the woman with the harp at the empty spot where King Billy used to stand. Frank let his hands drift lower. He traced the outline of my knickers through my skirt, lightly, like he was playing the stringed harp himself; it could have been almost angelic the way he twanged that elastic against my arse.

'Light-fingered, still, are you?' I said to him, but I

couldn't help smirking as we swerved and slid down a wee lane, heading towards a squat, grubby pink building. Yes, now he'd pulled me off the street and away from the traffic my heart was beating a jig in my chest and I thought for a moment he might push me up against the wall like he used to, fire into it straight away. Have me with my back to the graffiti, under the blue streetlights, one leg lifted and my well-oiled crack swallowing him gladly.

But there was something nervy about him. He looked all about as we reached the corner and I thought to myself: first, where the hell is it we're going; and, second …

'God, are you ashamed to be seen with me? You, Frank McAuley, a once-upon-a-time pony kid from Finglas with dirt under your nails?'

I was about to shout him off when he tugged me into the narrow gap between the germolene-pink roughcast and this big ungainly crate of a van that was parked arse backwards on the pavement.

'Hoy!'

The voice, spraying out of the darkness, was dog-harsh, and all my skin swarmed with sudden fright. But Frank was patting me down and nosing towards the sound. For a moment I wished he were less of a swaggerer. He'd always been inclined to get us tangled up in mischief, and never one to shy away from a bare-knuckle scrap, either.

'S'dat you, Eddie? How's it going?' Frank sounded oddly cheerful.

There was a low grumble, and the sound of someone clearing their throat and howking a great gob into the gutter.

'McAuley. Where the fuck've yow been?'

The voice was fat, and as my eyes adjusted I saw that it belonged to an appropriately gigantic great fucker standing in a doorway. One of those that manage to menace just by the set of their shoulders. Frank shrugged.

'Oh, just catching up with me old friends, Eddie. All work and no play, Eddie, know what I mean?'

Frank smacked me then, hard on the behind, and I yelped before I could stop myself, despite the fact we hadn't agreed to that kind of a scene, not yet at any rate, and that Frank was giving a lewd, guttery chuckle that made me want to snap the fingers off his hand. And I would have too, if I hadn't been so wary of the sumo wrestler standing but six feet from us and stinking of bad news.

'Niamh, meet Eddie,' Frank said, pushing me reluctantly forwards until I could smell the man's breath. I got a whiff of blackcurrant throat sweets under the stale smoke and black coffee. Eddie breathed on me a bit more, assaulting me with halitosis, before turning back to Frank.

'I don't like you hanging around here, Frank. And you've parked your knacker's wagon too fucking close.'

'Can't grudge a fella a few scoops and a quick ride, surely, Eddie? Hold your hour, eh?'

Eddie glowered.

'You'll be on the last ferry, Frank.'

'Aye, course I will. Swear on my grandmother's grave.'

Another grunt, and the man-mountain receded into a doorway that was a patch of darkness against the wall's vivid pink.

I could almost hear Frank's shoulders relax. There was a glint in the dusk that might have been a flash of his teeth if he were smiling at me, and he moved up against the side of the caravanette. A moment of him fumbling and swearing, and I realised that he was fiddling with keys. He swung open a dwarf-sized door and held out his hand.

'Want me to carry yer over the threshold?' he asked, and he had that quirky grin on his face, the one he used to use when he'd been out all night and was in the mood for playing up. He'd meet me outside my bedsit and drag me off into the dark, soot-blackened labyrinth of the city, talking a mile a minute, eyes shining with speed or lust or whatever devious scam he was working on at that present moment.

And I'd let him tangle his fingers into my hair and kiss me. And I'd let him drag me wherever he was going, just like I did then. Up the rickety steps and into the interior, smelling of biscuits and air freshener and damp towels.

He flicked a switch and a weak, yellowy overhead light dripped from the ceiling.

Everything was beige. It was like I'd gone back twenty years to a simpler, browner time; before everyone I knew I wore white-soled dubes and talked about irony and house prices. I was about to ask what the fuck we are doing in the bachelor pad from hell, when I realised how close Frank was standing, and suddenly it didn't really matter any more. There was another thing that was familiar, and that was the way his eyes shifted out of focus as he leaned in to kiss me.

That mouth. It might have produced some of the filthiest lies you've ever heard in your life, but there's no denying that when Frank McAuley kissed you, it was enough to make St Peter forgive the devil. He tasted of whisky and wet nights on the town, he covered my lips with his own and devoured me, drew me forward so it felt like I was falling. I banged my shin against some clutter on the floor, swayed against a hard edge and knew I'd be bruised.

Around us the caravan creaked and swayed. Frank bent his head and bit into my neck, pushing me back until I put out my hands and felt the clammy plastic surface of a table and gripped it. A magic tree hung from the rear-view mirror, smelling of sickly synthetic vanilla. It swung back and forth in time with his movements.

Frank drew his tongue over the pulse point in my throat and flicked at my collarbone. He jammed his leg between mine and rocked closer and closer to my groin. Always quick on the advance, Frank. Still, I couldn't pretend I didn't like it. I had to press my lips hard together to stop myself from groaning.

'Dat's it, girl,' Frank murmured, nuzzling lower, pushing my jacket aside, burrowing into the dark, soft places where he chased my pulse with kisses. I whimpered.

'You like that, Niamh? Will you sing for me, eh?' He found my breast with his finger and squeezed it tightly, plucking at my nipple until I let out a long, loud sigh. Pleased, he gave a soft laugh and tweaked it harder. Sadist.

'God, I missed you,' I said, through gritted teeth.

'Been pining for me?' he murmured, slipping his head down to suckle me through my dress. With one hand, he worked his way up my thighs, incy wincy spider. I opened my legs.

'Oh, you're impatient still, Niamh.'

His hand withdrew.

Of course he wouldn't give me the satisfaction. Not Frank. Not that easily.

I moaned.

'You fucking big tease, Frank'.

He kissed my earlobe, bit into the tender flesh, and my knees sagged.

76

'I don't have any johnnies,' he said. 'I wasn't presuming this would happen, d'you know.'

'That'd be a first,' I murmured. I looked around the shabby interior, as if there might by some divine ordinance be a contraceptive vending machine installed in it.

'I'll nip out,' Frank said, licking his lips. His eyes tripped down to the wet patch on my dress where he'd left teeth marks. 'But I want to make sure you're still here when I get back.'

I shrugged. 'Can't promise anything.'

'Oh, I know that.' He started sliding my jacket down my arms, and I stood dumbly while he plucked at the buttons on my dress.

'You think it's time I slipped into something more comfortable, so?' I said, bemused.

'Not exactly,' was his answer, and as he roughly stripped my dress from me and left me shivering in my underwear, I got a sudden pang between my legs. I recognised that tone.

'I don't know if I'm in the mood for games, Frank.'

'You'll like this one.'

He unpeeled my stockings – tugging them off my legs with less finesse than I'd imagined when I rolled them on earlier – and rolled the nylon around his fists.

'Lie down,' he said, nodding towards a bunk bed at the back of the caravan.

I lifted an eyebrow.

'For old time's sake,' he said, 'lie down,' and his voice was a soft growl. It made me wet.

I did as he said. While he tied my hands to a cupboard door handle above my head and my ankles tight together, I found myself staring at a water stain on the ceiling. It was in the shape of a map, perhaps, a country that no one had ever been to before and no one else would ever notice.

Frank was quick with the knots. He knew how to fix me in the right position. From our left came a sudden burst of muffled noise. Music. Some loud, hard beat. Frank looked up.

'Ah, that's the club kicking off,' he said, 'The night's just beginning.'

He smiled at me as he pulled my knickers halfway down, leaving my fanny shockingly exposed. His eyes lingered. He hesitated, and then with one quick movement, he bent down and thrust his tongue between my legs, giving me one big gasp of a lick from arse to clit – the kind that makes you breathless.

'Got you goin'?' he asked, smacking his lips. I rolled from side to side.

'Do it again.' I tried not to let it sound like I was begging.

'Not for now.' He tucked my hair behind my ears and ignored me as I squirmed from side to side. 'You be a good girl, now, and wait here for me and I'll be back soon enough and give you the fuck of your life.'

I blushed. When he said things like that, I could feel his cock in me already, like he could penetrate me just with his words.

He looked over his shoulder.

'I tell you what, though, Niamh. You wouldn't want big Eddie coming by and thinking you were on your own in here, would you?'

My eyes got wide at the thought.

'Don't you fuckin' even dare think about it, Frank.'

'Shh,' he said, laying a finger on my lips. 'Oh, hush, I wouldn't. I'm just saying, for your own comfort, like, it might be best to act like I was here.'

'How d'you mean?'

He nodded at me. 'Roll around some, you know. Give it a bit of the groaning like you do.'

'Groaning?'

'You know, a few oohs and ahhs. Put on a wee show for old Eddie, like.' Frank tweaked my nipple until I arched my back.

'Ahhh,' I said, predictably.

'That's the one,' he said, his smile twisting just as his fingers were. 'I'll be back in the blink of an eye.'

And he left me, tits smarting, pussy craving, bound hand and foot and trying pathetically to wriggle around and rub myself off on the sticky nylon bristle of the couch. I didn't even have to pretend – never mind who was outside. I'd been turned on and left to simmer and nothing was going to calm me until Frank McAuley got back and made good on his promise. I bit my lip and dreamed of his long-forgotten cock, growing bigger and stiffer and more beautiful by the minute.

God, and it was hard to leave her like that. The ties, now they always did suit her. Black nylon against that soft white skin. Like a bowl of cream, she was, even after ten years in the birl and bluster of the city. Sweet. I could still taste her on my lips, which, right enough, I couldn't stop chewing.

Nervous habit. No one would blame me for the nerves, even though I could have used a steady hand right at that moment, holding the drill tip hard up against the safe so that it wouldn't slip. The sweat on my hands didn't help. Eddie's office was a dingy little hole the temperature of hell itself; I reckon the body heat from two hundred shitfaced clubbers must have been seeping in through the walls. And fuck-all breeze from the fire escape, either, even through the broken door that I'd propped open behind me.

I'd to wait, every so often, for the music to slide from melody into thumping bass, so's no one would hear the groan of the drill. And then the air was thrumming with music and I could bend to my task, gritting my teeth against the fearsome smell of hot metal, watching tiny bright corkscrews curl out of the holes and scatter over the floor.

Eddie would be lurking in his doorway listening to Niamh's performance. God, the noises she makes! Purrs like a kitten. Enough to make my knob twitch just thinking of it. And that fat-headed cunt never could resist a peepshow.

Concentrate, Frank. That's three holes now, just another dozen or so and the lock'll come loose. There's just inches between me and a glorious bonus that I'll be keeping all to my grand wee self. I'll be free of my curse and those nasty shites who'd laughed like scuttling drains all me life – soundtrack to my grim fucking childhood, their laughing – oh, they'll be stuck, won't they? Left with a big box full of fuck all, and me halfway across the Irish Sea already with the gear tucked nicely away and my balls aching sweetly.

They thought they had the measure of me, still. Thought I was just a thick-headed mule, the type that would scare with their fat necks and insinuations and the slightest crack of their grazed knuckles.

Jesus, what's that? That great croaking sound? A door?

Calm yourself, Frankie boy. Doors open and close, that's what they do, doesn't mean anything much. Doesn't mean Eddie is coming back this way; why would he, when he's got a club to run and his money all tucked away in here safely behind an inch of solid steel? Who'd expect dumb wee Frankie would have the nous or the clackers to bring along a drill, eh? Who'd expect he'd know to use a cobalt bit at slow speed?

Aye, if there's one thing I am grateful to Her Majesty for, it's the useful skills she taught me in the metalworking shop. Getting there, now. Eight holes. I can practically smell the fucking lucre.

Dreamed of her a few times, when I was inside. Niamh, I mean. The ginger-coloured curls of her cunt, as snug and cosy a place as I'd ever longed for. Yes, she knows how to present herself, does Niamh. Give me fifteen minutes, and by god I'll be drilling a new hole right in the hot wet centre of her.

Fortune favours the bold, they say. But then there's a thin line between the bold and the bloody stupid.

If Frank McAuley had listened to the blacksmith who sold him the gear, he'd have realised that the batteries needed to be charged for fully twenty-four hours before he used the cobalt-tipped drill.

And if the drill had not slowed, with a pathetic, weakening whine, just as he was halfway through making the tenth hole, while he was lost in dreams of Niamh's dear warm wetness, Frank may not have shouted his dismay quite so loudly. His cry, unfortunately timed, just cracked through the silence between two tracks when the air was still throbbing with the echo of bass.

Eddie, waiting out in his shadowy doorway with one eye on the queue of punters and the other on the gently rocking motorhome, heard the agonised, distant wail coming from deep in the bowels of the club.

A frown gathered and settled on his forehead like a small rain cloud.

He looked at the Laika. For the past fifteen minutes

he'd listened to the various whimpers and growls, muted but pleasant nonetheless, that emanated from the decrepit old van. They were entertaining enough to keep him out here with his hands in his pockets, waiting while the club filled up.

But he could have sworn that howl of anguish coming from the direction of his office was that snivelling little gobshite Frank McAuley. He'd listened to the bastard crying for mercy often enough in the good old days. The pitch was familiar.

Eddie walked closer to the Laika. The net curtains were drawn closed, and he couldn't see the ghost of a thing. He licked his lips. She had a fine rack on her, that betty Frank had dragged back.

Clutching at his balls, Eddie leaned in close as if he could smell whether there was a man in there or not. He put a hand against the thin metal wall. There was a sharp intake of breath, and the moans broke off.

'Frank?'

Jesus, she sounded all but desperate. The sound of a woman with the raging horn – enough to break yer heart.

'Frank, is that you?'

Eddie looked over his shoulder. His mind moved like tectonic plates; with geological slowness to begin with, but with eventual cataclysmic consequences. Behind the restless queue of young D4s forming at the raspberry pink wall, there was a fire exit, and behind the fire exit there was a corridor. Along which, Eddie's inner sanctum. Eddie licked his lips.

If Frank was stupid enough to be attempting what Eddie thought he might be, he was tucked away in there, fiddling with a safe that, to be honest, would hardly hold up if you farted on it.

Eddie was only holding the cash here for this one

night, of course. By tomorrow, it would be counted and split and distributed to various laundries around the republic. Nobody wanted to keep that amount of money in one place for too long. It only leads to trouble.

'Ah, Frank,' Eddie sighed. He really couldn't be arsed with this.

'God's sake, would you get in here,' the girl hissed. 'The circulation's going in my wrists.'

Eddie raised an eyebrow.

It had been six months, minimum, since he'd had any hole. People thought a man like himself would have whores buzzing round him like flies round honey, but those times were long gone. They'd all read too many women's magazines now, they all thought they were fucking *worth it*. And, despite what many of his friends thought, he wasn't inclined to pay for it. Deep inside Eddie's craven bulk there was a soft, sentimental heart that wanted a good Catholic girl with a bit of pink in her cheeks and the ability to *smile* while she sucked your cock.

He climbed the rickety little step, reached for the door handle and turned it slowly. About as secure as the tin-can safe Frank was currently trying to break into, he reckoned. Inside smelled of damp weekends. There was another smell, too – the smell of an impatient woman. Eddie's eyes searched the half-gloom. He moved across the room.

Niamh was spread-eagled on the bed, tits and fanny all bare-naked and hanging out for anyone to see. The blush ran to Eddie's cheeks, and he gritted his teeth, keeping his eyes fixed on her wide, terrified eyes.

'Christ.'

The girl gasped. Eddie's hand swayed for a moment over her chest, which heaved and bucked, although he hadn't laid a finger. Swiftly, he pulled the curtain down and draped it over her, covered her from her chin to her knees with dingy white lace.

'Jesus. What has he done to ya?' Eddie asked, shaking his head.

'Frank,' the girl said, almost whispering. 'Where is he?'

She was a looker, Eddie thought. Classy bird, with that haircut. Probably drank white wine and read proper books. Wonder if she knew any of those fancy kinds of sex tricks he heard about but never actually encountered. You know, European type stuff. He ran a hand through his slicked-back hair.

'Frank?' He made it sound like a swearword. 'My guess is he's currently trying to rob me.'

Niamh frowned. Her hands were still tied, but she balled her fists and tugged against the rope.

'Get me out of this,' she said. Eddie shook his head sorrowfully.

'Sorry darlin'. Not just yet.'

Eddie allowed himself to glance at the outline of her breasts under the lace curtain. For a moment he swayed between lust and common sense. Then he cleared his throat, roughly.

'What's his plan, so?'

'Who, Frank's? How the fuck would I know? Do I look like his PA?'

Eddie scowled. She'd a mouth on her. Slowly, deliberately, he took his knife out of his back pocket and knocked it against the table edge before prising it open. To her credit, the girl didn't even flinch. She just opened her eyes wider, till you could see the whites. Only the goosebumps on her bare arms gave her away.

He started to clean his fingernails with the tip of the

knife.

'How should I know you're not colluding?' That Frank, he hasn't the brains of a dead haddock. We both know that.' Eddie concentrated intensely on his thumbnail.

'So, maybe he needed someone to tink up a plan like this. Someone with a bit o' nous.'

'What plan?' She actually snapped at him. She did.

Eddie nodded at the bed on which Niamh lay. 'Yer arse,' he said pleasantly, 'is lain on a mattress on top of a rather large parcel of quality cocaine. The money for which, Frankie brought me last night. And as we speak he is in my office trying to rob it back.

'Now Frank is after the drugs, the money and the vengeance,' Eddie continued, 'and I'm wonderin if you're Bonnie to his Clyde.'

'The gobshite.' Niamh slammed her head back against the mattress. 'The dirty great scheming lying cock-awful gobshite. I should have listened to my mother. I should never have let my hormones get the better of me.'

Eddie allowed himself a smile. He knew guilt like an old friend, inside out and up and down, and Niamh's was not the reaction of a guilty woman. As he reached for the nylon stockings with the blade of his knife, he wondered, idly, what the best way would be to punish a ratface fucker like Frank McAuley.

At least, when the drill ran out, Frank didn't waste too much time kicking the safe. He'd only sprained his big toe before he realised he was onto a losing game, and that he'd less time than a priest's wank to clear out of the place and get back to the Laika.

Breathing hard, he reassured himself. So he didn't have the money, but he did still have the goods, wrapped and bagged nice and tight under the bench where Niamh was tied.

Frank opened the door of the office a crack and checked the corridor. Oh, she was a fine bit of woman, that Niamh. He'd forgotten, in truth, just how much she wound him up. What an arse she had.

He'd only to wait for the next song now, something loud enough to cover the sound of the door scraping open. He craned his neck around the corner. The place was empty but for scuffed footprints on the lino and a few crushed fag butts. The walls in here were oxblood red, about the same colour as Neve's lips in the deep centre. Frank remembered how he'd left her, pliant and willing and begging for it. He slid along with his back to the wall, one eye on the door through to the bar. His heartbeat thumped so loud it almost drowned out the steady drone of the music. But no one appeared. Breathing hard, he reached the fire exit, propped open with an empty beer bottle. He could smell the yeasty mix of Dublin's night air, the cigarettes and laughter and the thousand jokes that mingled on the warmed-over sea breeze.

As he scurried along towards the Laika, keeping on the outside where the shadows were darkest, Frank added up in his head. Would he have time, yet, to finish what he'd started with Niamh, and still catch the last boat? Was it worth the risk?

His cock twitched in his trousers, and he could almost hear it reason with him like a little devil-voice. Burn off the adrenaline, wouldn't it? Almost make up for losing out on six hundred odd grand. He smiled as he reached the driver's door, and pulled it open with a rush of relief.

Primed for a swift, stunningly satisfying shag, Frank climbed into the cab of the Laika with a filthy great smile on his face. So when he went through to the back and failed to notice that the overhead lights were now out, he maybe dived a little too quickly towards the banquette where his oblivious, sweetly horny ex girlfriend was trussed up waiting for him.

Only as he groped for a breast did he realise, with a slowly growing sense of horror, that the chest he was feeling was hairier than his own.

You know, the Irish fellows never fail to surprise me. I might never have believed that Dublin's second hardest gangster was capable of the gentlemanly restraint that Eddie showed as he untied me and sat at the table, respectfully turning his back when I asked for some privacy to dress.

Perhaps nobody would ever have thought Eddie for the type to turn his back on anyone, least of all a woman with a temper and an unresolved orgasm. But he did, meek as a choirboy, and allowed me time to lift the mattress and find the satchel and get a good swing at him. I'd only to lamp him the once. Force equals mass times acceleration, as we all know.

And perhaps no-one would have thought that I, Niamh Carmichael, with the bobbed hair, the good job and yoyos to spare, would have the gumption to take not only the satchel full of cocaine, but also, by way of getting a simple answer to a simple question that I asked Eddie nicely – though I admit I'd to slap him awake and hold his own pocket knife to his big sweaty bollocks right enough – get the combination of the safe, easily slip into the club by flashing my lipstick smile at the bouncers, and collect the money in the safe – a large sum but not too large to fit in my handbag, no, not the roomy leather one I'd splashed out a week's wages on – before scarpering in a taxi, so, for the last ferry, and freedom, and even if nobody believed it and wondered where I'd got to, and whether I was at the bottom of the Liffey, it didn't matter so much.

No, I thought as I looked out over the Irish Sea towards fresh horizons. Home was home, and sometimes that was a good enough reason to leave. I thought of Frank and Eddie, stuck in that foul little caravan under the streetlights, and raised a glass to toast them.

'May the devil make ladders of your backbones while he's picking apples in hell, boys.'

About the Story

MY FIRST TIME IN Dublin I was with a black-haired blue-eyed man full of all that rough charm the Irish do so well. I remember all the deep, vivid, acid colours of the place and the cobbles and the fights we had.

Dublin seemed to be two cities at once – an actual stone and brick city with a river and locals and traffic and that beautiful song-like accent floating about everywhere – and the simulacrum of Dublin overlaid (or perhaps rather plonked on top). So there were shops with velveteen emerald green leprechauns and Guinness hats and shamrock-bedecked tat jostling alongside the self-conscious hipness of Temple Bar and the new Euro-cool atmosphere blending with the hugely rich history and culture of the place.

I wanted to try and convey that sense of a city with different faces – Frank being the prodigal returning and unsure of whether he misses the place or loathes it, Niamh being the adopted Dubliner whose relationship to the city hovers between pride and frustration.

I suppose because the story is so rooted in its location I ended up exploring the idea of home as somewhere we can love and loathe at the same time; whether it's comfortably awful or horribly pleasant. Niamh and Frank's affair is an echo of that idea; old flames that are guaranteed to be more trouble than they're worth, yet remain an irresistible temptation.

I hope I've managed to capture something of the city, or at least how I've experienced it and its people. I wanted to get that daring dash, the deeply roguish quality that I remember from the times I've spent there, mixed with a thread of black humour and a nip of something strong and illicit.

Molly, You Have 4391 Words, Start Now …
by Maxim Jakubowski

… AND I GAZED AT the drunkards roaming up and down Lower O'Connell Street at midnight, and gusts of wind were directing empty, dirty moulded yellowish polystyrene containers stained with ketchup and strands of wet lettuce, on a twisting journey, floating between kerb and pavement, and I almost stumbled over a rogue piece of detritus as it caught my heel, and I don't know why but it made me think of my French lover and I sighed.

I had been here for almost six months now, and still I couldn't banish him from my mind.

Why him? Why now?

Maybe these were the Primark shoes I had worn on the last occasion we had spent together. Or maybe not? Four-inch heels, deep blue silk-like fabric, thin straps gripping ankles. Elegant and practical.

'Hey, darling,' another inebriated bastard shouted at me, stumbling out of an all-night convenience store, clutching a bottle of some foul beer in a paper bag in his left hand, 'need company, pretty one?'

I ignored him and moved on, without a further glance at the guy, in the direction of the river; the Liffey that somehow always smelled to me of Guinness and faded hopes. Go figure.

But that fleeting memory had again flared up inside me, and all of a sudden the wetness in my cunt felt like a fire, expanding outwards from my sexual epicentre like a blaze out of control.

I halted my steps for a minute or so, stood still, attempting to regain my composure; even if it meant that I now looked to others from a distance like yet another Saturday night drunk on the lash. Another Dublin woman of easy virtue.

Oh yes, right then, all shreds of my innocence were long gone and buried. Standing there, trying to repress the insidious heat coursing through my insides, I could feel the clamminess inside my cunt, the private secretions beginning to pearl slowly down my thighs and possibly staining my skirt in all too visible areas. The come of men, the seed of strangers.

Just five minutes ago, I had made my way through the over-lit lobby of the Gresham Hotel, dodging the possibly inquisitive looks of the night staff, emerging into the warm night. Could they tell from my face, the deep sheen of my eyes, that I was freshly fucked? I wondered. He used to tell me, back in those glorious days, that, after we had made love, my eyes could not conceal the fact. They shone, he said. Like diamonds. Or was that only because I believed I loved him? Which was far from the case with the men I'd just left behind in that hotel room. They had no faces, no names, just cocks that had used me thoroughly while I lay there almost like an observer, passive, sluttish, damaged.

I had met them in a pub near Trinity College. I was feeling lonely, almost on the verge of tears and drink was not enough of a solution. One of them had approached me, and I had in a daze stumbled through the mechanics of social communication, accepted another drink, then a second one, and he was joined by two friends. 'My name is Molly,' I'd told them, 'I'm studying here, on an Erasmus exchange programme. I'm from Seattle.' Fact is my name is anything but Molly, although the rest was true. Well, this was Dublin after all. None of them remarked on the literary association, not that I expected them to.

I nodded, smiled feebly, never quite said no as weak jokes quickly turned into overtly indecent suggestions, and an hour later found myself in the room at the Gresham, smuggled through the large reception area towards the bank of lifts and transported down unending corridors, with hands roaming across my rump, to the scene of the crime.

… and all too soon the words ceased and it all became a clandestine world of grunts and instructions and aggression; savage lust unleashed and that familiar disorienting blend of being lost, pleasure, guilt, and downright humiliation, and there were faces blank and grimacing, littering my often restricted field of vision, and landscapes of bare skin in the unforgiving penumbra of the hotel room, fingers lingering all over my body, touching me, pinching me, invading me everywhere, pulling at my limbs, stretching me, forcing my limits. Oh yes, there were cocks, taking turns in all my holes, the redolent taste of dried urine invading my mouth, of hanging, hairy ball sacks whipping my chin and my arse cheeks as all three men took turns fucking me in turn and then together as they conjured up further positions which could allow them all to fit inside me at some point at the same time and my sinews screamed and my flesh expanded to extreme dimensions in the immediate periphery of my now bruised openings and I ran out of words and became a creature, an animal who could only express herself with dull grunts, moans, sighs, all obscene sounds that betrayed the absolute submission I had surrendered too. On the other hand the men were, in contrast with the piece of meat I had willingly become in this ritual of transformation, verbal and hungry, and they shouted at me, whispered in my ears, screamed with every new and painful and insistent thrust cutting me open, apart, oh yes they could effortlessly master all the right words in the thesaurus of copulation: 'bitch', 'cunt', 'slut', 'pig', 'whore', 'breed her', 'cow', 'slave', 'bag of bones', 'dog', 'piece of shit', 'slapper', 'take it deep, now', 'come on, gag on it', 'open up more', 'filth', 'suck', 'swallow', 'take that', 'lick me clean', 'stick your tongue in', 'girlie', 'foreign tart', oh they never did run out of things to say, as they crucified me and fucked me for hours. But it didn't matter to me that, escorted by these men whose names I didn't even know or wish to know, I had switched off from the very moment I had passed over the hallowed threshold of the Gresham Hotel, and had moved into that strange zone where I became just an observer and disconnected from my own body and mind. I had made myself available. Full stop. So it mattered not that after they had exhausted all the normal avenues of penetration, and I was dripping from every aperture, I was then ordered to lick the come dripping from me onto the carpet, or that one of the men sat on my face while the others held me stretched on my back over the ravaged bed and, dissatisfied with my tongue's efforts inside his crack then farted into my mouth while laughing his head off. Yes, there was pain when they twisted my nipples until they became red and sharp, or spanked me until I could not stop screaming or fisted me or spat in my face and one, the oldest I think, not that I can now even remember who was who or did what, finally dragged me, stumbling, to the bathroom and forced me into the bathtub and urinated all over me. Oh yes, this was not happening to me, but to another surely? A woman who had never enjoyed a French lover and known joy and a million epiphanies. The pain would go, the marks on my white skin would vanish, time would pass. There was no right and no wrong, no morals involved, just the yearning and the missing and unknowing what tomorrow would bring. I sat on the edge of the bed, sweat and come pouring from me, my hair in disarray, still obscenely open everywhere, panting and slightly out of breath from my exertions and their relentless attentions as the three men dressed, ignoring me, almost as if now embarrassed by my presence. 'Can I take a shower before I leave the room,' I timidly asked. One of them nodded indifferently and they slammed the door on me. Oh yes, another night in Dublin.

And now I was back on O'Connell Street, dancing an invisible waltz with the drunkards and the gently coasting McDonald containers littering the kerb like flowers.

And the night was still young.

Still badly wet between my legs, I ventured into a side street near the General Post Office and in a dark corner slipped off my dirty knickers; then hesitated a brief moment, wondered whether I should just stuff them into my small handbag, but then decided to just chuck them. I would never wear them again, would I? Lost in my thoughts of my French lover who once ordered flowers to be delivered to my door ten days in a row, which had my parents fuming and ever quizzing me as to my enterprising, and romantic suitor. Ah, the flowers, roses in white and red and pink, and their smell intoxicated me, and then one day he scattered dark chocolate amongst them, which melted inside my mouth with the sheer sweetness of his come and one night, lonely in my childhood bed, I even forced a square of the dark, fragrant chocolate into my cunt and allowed it to dissolve, fucking myself with its clinging butter, coating the pinkness of my innards, staining the sheets, surrendering to the wonderful madness of my French lover's crazy courtship.

A night breeze caressed my cheeks as I approached the river and crossed where Lower O'Connell Street morphed into Westmoreland once past Aston and Burgh Quay.

Oh yes, he had spoiled me rotten and beautifully. My French lover, like a sailor from Gibraltar returning from his journeys and I was his Penelope, laden with roses in all shades of the spectrum, chocolates, CD box sets, exotic teas, necklaces which he always insisted I wear for him in the bedroom when naked, a ritual. Oh, his cock, the veins pulsing down its thick trunk which my tongue would slavishly follow in its methodic and forensic exploration as I took him into my mouth until his mushroom stumbled across the back of my throat and I felt like gagging, and the smell of his body, of his balls, of his arse when he asked me to force a finger inside, of his piss blending with his pre-come as he leaked under the serenade of my lips. My French lover, my parachute, my very first lover, my professor of sex, oh yes, the furrows of his ball sack, the scars on his back, oh yes, he wanted to take me one day to New Orleans where he would show me the Mississippi and fuck me on a wrought iron balcony oh yes he would oh yes he should oh yes he would make me a bayou queen and feed me gumbo with a spoon and smear the jambalaya across my flesh and eat from my skin, spice me, flavour me, fuck me, eat me, fuck me, eat me, oh yes, and where was my French lover today, where oh where?

Held back by the bewitching maelstrom of my memories, I had walked past the quadrant of Trinity

College in a state of total oblivion.

The bright lights and shop windows of Grafton Street beckoned. I'd never liked this pedestrian enclave of consumerism. I couldn't afford most things anyway, but what irked me most was the fact that it didn't even feel like Dublin; it could have been any city in the world, same shops, same brands, same products, same indifference. I didn't linger. Emerged onto St Stephen's Green. I stopped for a moment. The men's abandoned come inside me had stopped seeping out, although my rear hole felt uncommonly raw.

A car cruised over towards my side of the pavement.

'Hey girl …'

Another faceless man behind the steering wheel of a metal grey BMW 318i Estate. Eyes full of hunger. He liked me. Could he guess that I no longer wore any undergarments under my thin skirt and blouse? Could he smell me?

'Hi.'

'Looking for company?'

I sketched a vaguely appreciative smile. His hair was graying. Just like the hair of my French lover, I reflected wryly.

'Maybe.'

'How much?'

I laughed.

'I'm free. Quite free.'

'Really?'

'Truly, madly, deeply.'

'Perfect.'

He would do. A cock is just a cock.

'What's your name,' the driver called out.

'Penelope.'

'Can I call you Penny instead?'

'Fine with me.'

'Want to jump into the car? Might be warmer.'

'No. I don't get into car with strangers.'

'So?'

No point in making matters any easier for him.

'Go park your car. I'll stay here for another 10 minutes or so. Wait.'

'Sure?'

'Of course.'

'You're not going to just piss off, Penny, are you?'

'Not unless it starts raining.'

Which was unlikely tonight. The dark skies were cloudless and it was almost a full moon up there.

'Deal.' He drove off in search of a legal parking space.

He was back within five minutes. Eager.

He was taller than I thought.

We smuggled ourselves into St Stephen's Green, as he helped me over the small fence, touching up my arse through the thin skirt as he did so, then following me over.

'Where?'

'Does it make any difference.'

'You're so right, Penny.'

He face fucked me on the bandstand. Then fucked me proper, from behind, on the small stone bridge, raising my skirt to my waist and adding his wetness to his earlier predecessors, pulling my hair bunched inside his fist brutally backwards with every contrary thrust, impaling me. He was thick, hard as rock, and his breath smelled of booze. He came fast, like a volcano, flooding me with unbearable heat and I could feel him dripping down my legs, the stream of come drifting down my spread thighs and staining my shoes. Then he collapsed over my back, his breath halting, savage sounds of lust still gurgling in the back of his throat. Embedded together for a moment in silence, unholy joined, we stood in silence, half supporting each other. He finally flopped out of me. Pulled his cord trousers up and then hesitated a second or two. Took hold of my hair again and ordered me into a kneeling position, my wet arse still exposed to the air with my skirt bunched around my waist. As I squatted, I could feel myself leaking like a fountain.

His hands guided my mouth to his cock still jutting from his unzipped trousers.

'Lick me clean,' he said.

'Please?'

'Yes, of course. Pretty please, Penny …' he chuckled.

As soon as his still humid and odorous cock passed through my lips, it began hardening again.

I diligently sucked him clean, from head to ball sack. He withdrew quickly from my mouth, visibly in no hurry to come again.

'Good,' he said. Offered me a cigarette.

'I don't smoke.'

'You're missing out, girl …'

I straightened up and rose to my feet and unrolled the creased skirt down my legs again. There were stains all over.

'Don't go, yet,' he said, menacingly. He smiled at me. 'Game for more?'

I was tired, but caution dictated I not leave yet. He threw the cigarette end over the bridge into the still night waters.

'Come,' he said, taking me firmly by the hand.

Bypassing Henry Moore's bust of Joyce we descended towards the bank of the small, shallow lake. The moon illuminated the whole landscape like a neo-realist film set.

'Strip,' the driver ordered me.

'It's cold,' I protested feebly, although I had already bowed to the inevitable. I had long lost control of the situation.

'Strip!' he repeated loudly.

The traffic in the distance felt miles away.

Once I stood in front of him naked, he grabbed my few fragile pieces of clothing and stretched them across the grainy sand of the lake bank.

'Lie down. On your stomach …Yes, that way … Now raise that sweet rump of yours, Penny dear.' I followed his peremptory instructions to the letter.

I heard him unzip himself behind me.

A nailed finger delved into my sphincter.

I heard him spit into his hands and he then massaged his saliva into my opening, testing the resistance of my anal muscles. Already breached several times at the Gresham today. No doubt visibly red, bruised and partially stretched. He licked his lips in appreciation.

'I see you like it there, my young bitch.'

And impaled me on his savage cock there and then on the banks of the lake in the Green, and the whole wide world ignored my pain and I screamed as he hurt me and tore me and gaped me to unholy proportions and used me and defiled me as only a man can do. He just never stopped and very soon I was only half conscious as my body responded to the systematic pounding with a strange disconnect, a form of detachment I often experienced in the throes of sexual pleasure (if pleasure it really was?). It was as if I was watching the whole scene from above, a supernatural voyeur witnessing the event as the stump of his cock dug deeper into me with every motion until my entrance was bleeding and servile and a receptacle for his rage, observing as he now pulled his belt out of his trousers' waist buckles and tightened it around my throat so as to control the bucking of my body as he fucked my arse, just enough to ride me and not quite to choke me and all I could think of, watching this strange movie, was how my French lover once took me there for the very first time and how gentle he was, taking absolutely ages to open me with tongue then fingers then his wondrous cock, playing with every nerve in my body like a wonderful musical instrument and I became a symphony no a concerto no still an oratorio or better a requiem mass until the fire of his love was unleashed deep into my stomach and I then later licked him clean and our combined unholy menu tasted of sugar and spices and oh yes my French lover said he would one day take me to Gibraltar where the flowers were sublime and New Orleans where the crayfish live and you can watch the fireworks explode over the Mississippi and Jackson Square at midnight on New Year's Eve and you can walk along Bourbon Street in shirtsleeves in the deep deep of winter. Oh, he did promise me all that and more and fuck I miss him fuck I want him fuck I need him …

I opened my eyes and the driver had departed, leaving me there sprawled helpless across the ground. The evening was cooling fast. I shivered. Rose unsteadily, my joints aching and other parts of my body still raw, sinews still stretched beyond endurance, synapses on fire, bare flesh bruised. I quickly picked my clothing up and dusted the few items as best I could and dressed. I must have looked a sight!

I left the Green. In a daze, both empty and full, a ghost of lust, dirty and tousled, on automatic pilot. Past the Civic Museum, up St George Street, beckoned by the silent call of the Liffey's peaceful flow, heading north like a siren on a homing beacon.

The right heel on my Primark pumps broke, and I

abandoned both shoes and continued on bare feet.

I reached the river and sat on a doorstep on Essex Quay, catching my breath, summoning my scattered thoughts, attempting to somehow make sense of it all.

What was I doing here? I no longer knew why I had come to stay in Dublin. A useless thesis about turn of the century Gaelic literature was just a poor excuse. After all, my academic area of expertise was web-based citizen's journalism. More like running away.

Damn, my throat was parched and I could still taste the bittersweet aftertaste of the driver's cock against the inner walls of my cheeks. I changed direction and made my way towards Temple Bar. I needed a drink. My stomach lurched as I stiffened my pace. Food too.

Yes, Temple Bar was the place to be. My panacea, my escape. Anonymous amongst the crowds again. Yes. The front of my skirt was badly stained. I ironed out a few creases with the back of my hand and only managed to spread the dirt over a larger area. Noticed I was still clutching wet earth inside my clenched fist. Maybe it would all go unnoticed in the dark, I hoped.

Sticking to the back streets in my small quest, I found myself facing Christ Church Cathedral where the locals went to hear the bells ring out at the turn of the year, a full-circle ringing peal he had taught me that, besides the magic of New Orleans, was yet another wonder. I had no intention of still being in the city by New Year's Eve. I must move on.

Some passers-by gave me strange glances. The gaze of men lingered, alternately disapproval and unbound lust.

My bare feet glided over the cobblestones. I headed towards Gruel where I always relished the roast turkey with stuffing and cranberry crammed into hot home-baked rolls.

With one hand, I checked the inside pocket of my torn skirt. My emergency fifty euros note was, surprisingly, still there. After I'd eaten, I barricaded myself in the loo and cleaned up as best I could. Combed the dirt from the lake's slope out of my thick, bushy curls and rearranged my skirt around my waist so that the worst indelible stains scattered across its fabric no longer betrayed their origin through actual location. All a bit crooked, but late at night in the joyous frenzy of Temple Bar no one would notice.

The night's bacchanalia was in full throw already, tribes parading up and down the street, girls with skimpy skirts unveiling their lower fleshy orbs, boys in tight tee-shirts and frayed jeans, boisterous, boastful, drunk by half and determined.

This is how my French lover had once described New Orleans' Bourbon Street to me, where music criss-crossed the road from side to side as duelling bands performed for the Yankee dollar, the smell of Cajun spices and stale beer mingling in unholy matrimony, and the criers stand outside the bottomless clubs and the crowd drains down the pavement like a river stumbling, sipping hurricanes in tall misshapen plastic glasses.

I closed my eyes and for a brief moment stood still before I was sucked up into yet another amorphous group of celebrating youngsters, a hand neglectfully grazing my rump, a leg entangling with mine, a woman with too much make-up and shockingly scarlet lips taking me by the shoulder, inviting me to join them in their nocturnal expedition. Aimless, caught up in this wave of loud humanity, I followed in their footsteps.

'We're on the pull, girl ...' someone shouted out at me.

Peals of laughter ensued.

In step with my newly acquired bosom buddies, I

retraced my steps towards the Liffey, crossed the river where another group, as dishevelled and merry as we were, joined us by some form of osmosis, and we all continued up O'Connell Street. A strange sense of the familiar. Past the Gate Theatre and finally landing in Parnell Square, across from the Writer's Museum.

The group we formed part of fragmented. Couples fading into welcoming darkness. Others staying together. The woman with the scarlet lips was sitting next to me on the stone balustrade. Her hand touched my cheek with uncanny delicacy.

'I like your legs,' she said. 'You have beautiful ankles.'

She bent over, took hold of my instep and appeared to be weighing me on some imaginary scale. I stretched my leg forward and my skirt shifted upwards across my thighs. She looked straight ahead and noted with a secretive smile spreading across her features that I was not wearing any underwear.

'Wow, girl. That's brazen,' she exclaimed.

'Lost them earlier,' I said.

Scarlet Lips chortled, set my foot down and approached me. Her breath warm across my cheeks.

'Kiss me,' she said.

I bridged the narrow gap separating our lips and kissed her.

She tasted of alcohol and cigarettes. One of her hands ventured across my breasts. Her body was warm. Oh well. I closed my eyes. Capitulated.

Thinking how my French lover had tasted, sweet and savoury both, hard as nails and sensitive, his breath heaving upwards from his lungs like a mighty wind that would subdue me in its victorious wake and oh he was good and oh he was mine and his touch was like a veil of spices spreading across my flesh, awakening every square inch of my surrendering body, playing me like a piano, every touch electric, every caress a terrible torture as he summoned my buried lust back towards the surface of my life, a primeval force I had long forgotten I owned, a web of ardent if contradictory desires concealed under the civilised veneer of the uncultivated fields of my skin and oh my French lover led that orchestra of the night like a virtuoso, my moans like wind instruments, my sighs like violins, my heart like a drum and the electric touch of his soft lips against my cunt and the stubble of his two-day beard teasing my perineum as his fingers delved with the cunning of a wizard inside every one of my openings and all I could say was yes yes yes my love *amore tesoro* my darling my professor of love and yes again to my French lover who bought me a vibrant red rose to plant in my hair like a gypsy when he took me to that restaurant on Bleecker Street and I would scream yes yes and jesus jesus jesus when he fucked me well and the windows were open and all the cities where we made love could hear me shout like a banshee across the wild roofs of night and every sheet we stained with our juices would turn into a sacred relic …

'You're not really into girls, are you, dear?' her voice interrupted my thoughts. Her red lips retreated from mine.

'No, not really,' I admitted. My indifference to her embrace had been self-evident.

'Pity,' she said, stood up and waved me goodbye.

I blinked.

Morning arrived.

About the Story

I'VE ONLY BEEN TO Dublin twice. On the first occasion, it was more of an instance of passing through from airport to train station in order to visit J.P. Donleavy for a curious afternoon of editing and smoked salmon sandwiches on his country estate before returning to the city late at night to find that my hotel had relinquished my room, and being forced to sleep in a miniscule room under the roof, overlooking the Liffey, before rushing to the airport again before the breakfast room had even opened. A fleeting visit indeed. The second occasion was longer and more enjoyable and coincided with New Year's Eve, which gave us good insight into local drinking customs along O'Connell Street, and inevitably, Temple Bar. On the first evening, we were invited out to dinner by local crime writers and friends John Connolly and Declan Hughes. There I was expecting an introduction to Irish cuisine, but curiously, they chose a curry house, albeit a classy one. But there was still a catch-up during the following days and a visit to the city at length, including the obligatory visit to the Guinness Brewery, particularly Ulysses, and a few hours in the now sadly closed Writer's Museum was a great reminder of how Irish writers have left such an unforgettable legacy.

I've already written a crime/fantasy story set in Dublin for an anthology and, this time around, there was no way I could not tender homage – although I recognise, in a somewhat harsh way – to Molly Bloom's soliloquy. Thus my own Molly was born, for her sexual Calvary, yet another lost soul amidst the many women adrift in my books and stories. It could only happen in Dublin in my own mind, and, reader, be perplexed when I confess that I strongly identified with the character for a million reasons. Expiation, redemption, walking on the wild side, love or sorrow? You can make up your own mind.

Abstract Liffey
by Craig J. Sorensen

'*YAR LEFT-HAHNDED.*'

A woman with long, wavy red hair stared at the brush suspended a couple inches from the canvas. 'Mmm hmm.' I resumed painting.

'Me too.'

'Mmm.'

'I like the colours you used. Brighter than they really are. Guess you need that though.'

'Huh?'

'Setting is kind of ... well ... plain.' She studied the scene then the painting.

'Are you an artist?'

'Ah, you are a Yank.'

I nodded.

'I couldn't do a proper job of painting a white wall.' She stepped closer to the painting. 'Where are the people?'

'What?'

'In the painting. Where are the people?'

'I'm doing a painting, not a photo. People move kind of fast.'

She chuckled. 'Just trying to figure out why you're painting the entrance of a shopping centre with no people.'

'Thought you weren't an artist.'

'I'm not.'

Her fair face was sprayed with freckles. One freckle in her pale lower lip looked like a piercing. She hooked her thumbs in her faded blue jeans.

'I'm trying to paint.'

'I'll leave you be.' She turned away.

'Wait. I mean, if you want to hang out …' Truth was I didn't know why I invited her to stay, but I felt compelled.

'I'll buy you a pint at the Stag's Head when you're done.' She patted my shoulder.

'Stag's Head?'

'The pub. It's not far. Ya never been?'

'No.'

'Just what kind of tourist are you?'

'The kind who's trying to paint.'

'So why are you chinwagging with the likes of me?'

I laughed and resumed painting.

Caireann set a pint of Guinness in front of me. She spelled her name, which was pronounced Karen.

I politely sipped a bit of the foam. 'I'm Sven Lundgren.'

'Oh? Good Swedish lad, are ya?'

'I wouldn't go that far.'

She winked, took a hearty drink, shook her long mane and pushed it to her back to expose large golden hoop earrings. 'So, where are you from in America?'

'Near Philadelphia.'

'Got shopping malls there, do they?'

'Of course. Why?' I took a deliberate sip.

'Just trying to figure out why you came all the way to Dublin to paint shopping –'

'I paint other things!'

She jumped melodramatically.

'I paint other things.' I softened my voice.

'*Joost fookin' with ya, lahd.*' She winked.

I became aware that her eyes were deep green. Suddenly my heart pounded as hard as when the Aer Lingus jet landed.

'So you came to Dublin to paint. Why Dublin?'

'What do you mean?'

'Don't artists usually go to Paris, or Venice, or Rome, or …' she bit her lip. 'Barcelona or something?'

'I hate to fly.'

Her head lifted like a periscope from the sea. 'Did you sail here?'

'Well, no. I flew. I mean, it's just that Dublin's closer.'

A big, wry grin. 'So it was easier to fly from Philadelphia to Dublin, than to Paris, which I'm sure is host to many lovely shopping malls?'

They say, in football of the American sort, that the best defence is a good offence. 'Why did you come up to me when I was painting?'

''Cause you're left-handed.'

'So we're sitting here, drinking a pint together, and for all you know, I might be an axe murderer –'

'*Now why woold you go mardering an ahxe?*'

I covered my mouth to camouflage a grin. 'We're sitting here together because we're both left-handed? You do know like ten percent of the world is left-handed?'

'I stopped because you're left-handed. We're having this drink because you come to Dublin and paint shopping malls without people, and now for the hope I'll see you murder an axe.'

'Oh, for fuck's sake.' I'd heard it on movies spoken with an Irish accent; I figured it would convey.

110

She donned a suddenly serious, attentive expression. 'So do you mostly paint buildings?'

'Yeah. There's some great architecture in Dublin.'

'You paint at Temple Bar?'

'Not yet.'

'Great shops, with people, there.'

'Thanks for the tip.'

'Buildings are made for people, you know.'

'I'm down with that. But they stand without people too.'

A fresh, wry grin. 'I sure hope so, can't have them falling down.'

'Christ you're weird.'

'You reckon? So, you ever paint people?'

'As a student, sure.'

'You look at me like an artist studies a model.'

'Oh, I'm sorry. It's just that there's some ... thing you remind me of.' It was incredible how much.

'A thing, am I?'

'Sorry, someone.'

She winked. 'Who is it I remind you of?'

'I don't want this to sound wrong.'

'You worry about things that sound wrong hanging with the likes of me?'

I laughed. 'Guess not. You remind me of my first girlfriend.'

'You fancied her?'

'She was my girlfriend.' I said it like *duh*.

'What happened?'

'You know how these things go. First girlfriend, first love.'

'Tell me.' She cupped her chin, thumb and index finger resting in her deep dimples. Such a beautiful smile rendered with such ease.

I, by contrast, fumbled with consummate uncool. 'You think you … you like someone … you do … don't … you're … I don't know …' I finally blurted the explanation my mother had given like a sword-thrust. 'In love with being in love.'

'She broke your heart, didn't she?'

'Truth is, I broke hers.'

'Why?'

'Oh, you know how these things go.'

As we crossed the Ha'penny bridge into North Dublin, I turned toward the last gasp of sunset. The river Liffey was resplendent with reflections of yellow lights from windows, and purple and pink ribbons through the otherwise dark horizon.

'Feeling inspired?'

'Yeah, a little. I've always liked the way buildings look reflected in living water, the way the lights streak and mingle, kind of a natural abstraction.'

'I love abstraction.'

'I paint abstracts sometimes.'

She grabbed my elbow. 'Do ya? I'd love to see!'

'I've only done one since I came here. It isn't much.' I turned north, away from my uncomely, reasonably cheap room above a tea shop in South Dublin.

'Can I see?' She tugged south.

I tugged north, but she didn't budge. 'Oh, all right.'

'I love what you've done with the place.'

Paintings were strewn about, dishes and small pots piled in the small sink. 'Sorry.'

'It's an artist's place. I like it.' She stepped around a makeshift easel and studied a painting of a shop just down the road from the apartment. She moved gracefully around the clutter and continued to study.

'You said I look at you like an artist studies a model. Voice of experience?'

'I sat once or twice at university. You know, I'm not a big fan of architecture, but this is good.' She paused on a painting of the huge vaulted glass ceiling inside the St Steven's Green shopping centre and turned back. 'You and your shopping malls.'

'The ceiling there is fascinating. It just looms above, like a massive greenhouse, even a bit like ... the sky itself.' I quickly retrieved the one abstract wedged between paintings of a small local church and an old mansion. I made it a point that she saw I didn't just do malls and shops, then put the abstract on an easel.

She lit up. 'Makes me think of the sun.' She reached toward it then waited for my approval. I nodded and she traced the red aura, then its rim to the pale centre.

'Well, it is about warmth, comfort.'

'The shape is ... interesting. What are those?' She touched two green spots low in the painting.

'Trees ... I guess.'

'You guess?'

'Sometimes I just paint things ... you know, for feel. Grab a colour, put it down. I mean, it is abstract.'

'Oh, I meant no offence.' I'd never expected to hear those words.

'I'm not offended. Sometimes it's just hard to explain an abstract.'

'There's something kind of eerie, but comforting in it.'

I stopped and studied it to try to find out what she found eerie. She turned her eyes, but not her face, toward me. Caireann was flippant but deep. Intelligent but crude. She didn't wear make-up or perfume. There was something forbidden, but consumptive, about her. She

113

pressed her freckled shoulder to my upper arm and my cock perked up.

'You really get it … I mean, my painting.'

She turned her face toward me. I had to taste that freckle in her lower lip. She opened slowly, and I dived in like the first plunge from a high-dive. She lifted her arms and I broke the kiss just long enough to peel down her tank top. I fumbled with the snaps of her plain white bra. She reached around her back and flicked it open with her left hand.

From there, Caireann cooperated just enough. She folded her shoulders so I could peel her bra then shifted her hips so I could take down her jeans.

The ornate cross that dangled between her lean, shapely breasts amplified the sense of the forbidden. Perhaps it explained the pensive distance in her eyes which contrasted with her insistent kisses. Just like her lip, one of her pale nipples had a dark freckle amidst her Braille buds. I focused on that freckle. I guided her down to the bed and nearly ripped her panties off.

I delved into her with my fingers. She was sopping wet, silent with a hyper-aware gaze.

I needed her so badly, I stripped my clothes quickly, and entered her. She swivelled her hips in such a way as it bent my rod in her. It felt so good, and my orgasm instantaneously surged. I pulled out just in time to splatter up her stomach and chest.

She smiled as I swiped my load from her upper body. I finally cleaned the cross, which was like an iced Easter cake. 'I, uh –'

She tilted her head back toward the abstract. 'It's a face.'

'What?'

'Upside down, it's a face.'

I looked at the painting. 'No.'

'She's a redhead.'

'She? No, it's just a coincidence.' I threw my clothes on as quickly as I'd removed them.

Caireann went to the painting and turned it over. 'That's a chin. See that hint of a crease? Her mouth. The trees are her eyes. Her hair sweeps around her chin.'

'Maybe it's inspired by … by the stewardess on the flight over.'

'Stewardess?'

'Yeah, I was … well … I hate to fly, you know? Maybe her face … maybe she comforted … I mean … red hair … she did … you know … comfort me … made me feel more comfortable.'

'She had the green eyes?'

'Well … no … but who heard of a blue tree?' I half laughed, half cleared my throat.

'That girlfriend of yours had green eyes, didn't she?'

'No …'

'Did too.'

'Did not. Well … she's got nothing … anyway … it's just an abstract.'

'And you broke her heart?'

'I did!' I hated the way Caireann looked at me. Pity, disdain, whatever. 'Um, I gotta get up early …' I grabbed the front door handle.

She began to dress. 'You know –'

'Really early. Got a … a lot to do.'

Her shoes in her hand, she left. She didn't look back.

Five minutes after the door had closed, I felt horrible. She had been right, in her way. The break-up had been hard on me, and I took it out on Caireann for fathoming this. I had adored Lisa, from her long feet to her large, shapely nose, to her lively green eyes with the warm

115

spray of freckles on her cheeks.

I didn't know Caireann's last name or phone number.

I once read about a guy who dreamt the lottery numbers, awakened, played them and won. I knew there would be no lottery numbers now, but it was equally important that I focus. I knew this was indeed a dream, and it needed to be remembered.

The room was large or I was small. Probably both. I was seated, secured, could move, but couldn't, I was up high, but still so much above me. The setting was familiar, but I couldn't identify one thing in this place.

My mother's silver blonde hair hung straight down, slim lips, bright blue eyes, sandy skin. She grabbed things and put them behind me. I looked behind me, where she placed a colourful rectangle then turned back.

A red, dishevelled aura had replaced my mother's immaculate appearance. At the middle of the mass, speckles of warm rusty brown on ivory, bright pink lips, breath like candy canes. She looked cool to the touch but her soft palm rubbing my cheek was like a mitt fresh from pulling chocolate chip cookies from the oven.

The dishevelled woman said a few things, green eyes focused on me. My ears were muffled like I had marshmallows in them. She spoke to me like I was a person. I wasn't sure why that surprised me, maybe in my dream I was a dog. Then I realized my small fingers were wrapped around her thumb.

A sudden sting on my cheek, perhaps like being made to breathe after birth. The face before me was my mother again. She had a strange smile that wasn't really a smile. The red aura had disappeared.

When I awoke, I shuddered. I remembered that I'd had variations of this dream in my youth, but they had long since faded to black. This revival came with sparkling clarity, and I scribbled down every detail on a hunk of watercolour paper.

'Didn't get enough of this place before?'

I felt a warm chill up my spine. I rarely painted the same place twice, much less four times running, but it was the only thing I could think to do. I painted the entrance to The Royal Hibernian Way shopping centre day after day and stopped at the Stag's Head to choke down a pint on my way back to the flat each evening. 'I was hoping you'd happen by.'

'Really?'

'Yes, I was rude. I'm sorry.'

'You're a sweet lad. I figured … well, I'd overstepped.'

'You did. But it was a good thing. I mean, you're right. You may not be an artist, but you got a hell of an artist's eye.'

She winked. 'I'll give it back when I'm done.'

We walked along the south bank of the river until we reached the Ha'penny Bridge again. I was both relieved and disappointed when we reached the other side and turned to walk back along the other bank.

After one of our now customary long silences, she blurted, 'Did you know that the Royal Hibernian Way used to be a hotel? They tore it down back in the eighties.'

'OK?'

She shrugged. 'I'm just blathering. Still fascinated by your thing with shopping.'

Her comment sparked spontaneous expounding. 'I've painted abstracts similar to the one you saw for years.

Maybe inspired by a dream I used to have.'

'About your girlfriend?'

'No, the dreams were before that. After you pointed it out, what you saw in the painting …' I looked up in the bright blue sky. 'I had the old dream again.' I'd never told a soul about it.

As soon as I handed her the scrap of paper, I wanted to grab it away. I felt the same as I had in the plane before taking off from Philly. Caireann's right hand folded in to my elbow so I could guide her as she read, or maybe to anchor me from running. When she looked up from it, I spoke quickly, the way she usually did. 'Not long after my mother met Lisa, she told me it would never work between me and her. I asked why. She just said "she's not right for you", I said "but I like her, she's funny and warm". My mother, who was anything but passionate …' It took me a few moments to finish. 'She slapped my face so hard. I can still feel the sting. "Don't you defy me", she said. I was stunned.'

Caireann rubbed my razor stubble cheek as if to soothe the slap. 'What else?'

'What do you mean?'

'There was more, wasn't there?'

'No … yes … It's not important … I don't want to offend.'

Caireann lifted her red eyebrows.

I spoke in a compressed whisper. 'She said "You're worse than your father. I won't have you with that" …', I swallowed hard, '"Irish whore".'

'Aw.' Caireann bumped her shoulder to my arm.

'Lisa was so sweet. I was just … well … shit, I've never told anyone that.'

*　　　　　*　　　　　*

I sipped my Guinness the same way I had that first night. I wasn't getting any fonder of it but it wasn't for lack of trying. The place was removed from the Pub Crawl. The Victorian setting was relaxing, more locals than tourists.

I managed to nurse a pint to conclusion while Caireann polished off several. I thought she was going to say something, then she abruptly stood up. 'I've got an early day tomorrow. You know how to get back to your place from here?'

'Tomorrow is Saturday.' I took her hand. 'Maybe you could ... walk with me?'

'No.'

'I understand. I've got a bead on things. I'll find my way.'

I walked out slowly and waited for her to stop me. She didn't. I was a block west of the pub when I felt a warm hand on my elbow. 'Maybe ... I can't have you getting lost.' She turned me west, then north. We were absorbed into a series of streets, some straight, some curved. We turned with alarming frequency through rows of terraced houses. I looked around for landmarks, and knew full well we'd drifted far from the river. 'Are we going the wrong way?'

'No.' She stopped. 'Matter of fact, here we are.'

'Where?'

'My house.' She nodded at a brightly painted door. 'I've something I'd like to show you, if you have a moment.'

The living room had a couch facing a small fireplace with an iron insert and an ornate wooden mantle. The abstract above looked out of place with the simple, traditional furniture and architecture. Set back from the entryway door was a small alcove where a window opened on to the street. In this alcove, a wing chair with reading lamp partially obscured a colourful painting. I peered around the lampshade. The painting had elements of abstraction, blended with realism. It was clearly a woman's face. The freckle on the lip left no doubt. 'From your modelling days?'

'Modelling? Oh Lord, I was never a model.'

'But you said you posed –'

'Not for money. What artist would pay a ganky lass like me?'

'Ganky?'

'You know, ugly.'

'Christ, you're anything but ganky, Caireann.'

'Thanks, but I can be a bit … unpleasant.'

'Not at all. So who did the painting?'

'A friend.'

'Really?' There was a needful passion in the artist's hand.

'He used to call me Carrie-Ann. Goofy bastard.' She walked through the living room to the kitchen. 'Care for a drink?'

I stepped closer to the painting, touched the impasto strokes. The guy was good. 'Just a friend?'

'You paint buildings without people. He painted people without buildings. What are you drinking?'

'How long did you know him?''

Her voice got impatient. 'Long enough. Now what do you want?'

'Just water. He broke your heart, didn't he.'

'Water, just water?'

'He broke … your fucking … heart … Carrie-Ann.'

'*Fooker*.' She set a glass of water at one end of her couch and drank a bottle of Guinness deliberately and acted like she was ignoring me. She stared at the inert fireplace as if it were glowing. I remained where I was.

'Will you come away from that ganky thing?'

'I told you, you're not ganky. You're an absolute ride.' I even added Irish inflections and a Caireann-approved wink.

She grabbed her mouth and her cheeks flushed red. But within a moment her face was so sombre, even sad. I wanted her to light up with flippant comments. I goaded her with talk of shopping malls and fear of flying.

She responded politely, pensively. She became increasingly distant.

'Do you want me to go, Caireann?'

'No, please.' She patted my hand. 'Been thinking about your dream.'

'Oh?'

'Do you really not get what it means?'

'No, I don't.'

She lifted one brow.

'I don't.'

'Do you want to?'

'Of course.'

'Do you worry, if you know what makes you tick it might change … you know … how you view things? Art, whatever?'

'Whatever?'

'You know.'

'I don't worry. If my outlook on art changes, it'll be for the better.' I couldn't have been surer of myself.

'OK. Your father left when you were young. Why?'

'I don't know.'

'I'm not gonna tell you the bloody answer, you gotta meet it halfway. What does your ma not like about you?'

I began to fidget. 'Well, she says I'm like my dad.'

'And what don't you like about her.'

'I don't … do … don't … I mean, do like her fine.' I

looked around the room quickly.

She lifted an eyebrow.

'OK ... she is kind of cold.'

'What happened with the woman in your dream? What did you do?'

'I grabbed her thumb.'

'And what happened next'

I looked at the floor.

'Now, why do you think your father left your mother?'

I had the same urge to run as I'd had when she read about my dream, when she saw the face in the painting. I cleared my throat. 'She ... she's cold.'

'What do think he left her for?'

'Someone warm ... like ... the woman in the dream. Maybe ... mom met her ... and was mad because I touched her ... or smiled at her ... or liked her.'

'Or all of the above.'

I felt an electric charge up my spine. My heart raced as it all came together. 'Oh fuck.' I wanted anything to take away the focus I felt on me. 'I ... you do understand a lot about people.'

'I have a degree in psychiatry.'

'You're a psychiatrist?'

'No, I have a degree. I'm an office manager.'

'After all those studies?'

'My bedside manner is lacking just a wee bit.' We had been so serious that the convulsive laugh we shared was almost absurd. 'Anyway, after your ma –'

I practically jumped across the cushion and kissed her. I tugged at the base of her T-shirt as my tongue deepened like a hard, needful cock. She raised her arms. I realized, just like the first time we'd been together, this seemed like surrender. It didn't feel right, so I squeezed her waist until she let her arms fall to my neck. After the kiss, she studied me awkwardly.

'Maybe I better go now.'

'It's late. You should stay. I won't say any more about the dream.'

'No … it's not … I mean …'

There was that grin.

'Thanks, lass.'

'You're welcome, lad.' She kissed me.

We peeled off our clothes a piece at a time. I hooked my thumbs in my underwear, she held her hand at the clasp on the back of her bra.

After a tense pause, I pulled my underwear down then covered my semi-erect cock.

She released her bra, crossed her arms.

My cock came to full length. I let my hands fall to my sides.

She pulled down her panties and we crawled into bed together. I traced my middle finger along her collar bone. 'I'm glad you asked me to stay.'

She brushed my hair from my eyes with her left hand, then combed around my scalp. 'You're very handsome.'

'But?'

'But nothing. I like being with you.' I could not get a fix on the resignation in her face. She rubbed her silvery smooth nose to mine. The only sounds in the room were wet kisses, our hands became more familiar, stroking arms and ribs and stomachs.

I turned her on her back and lingered at her breasts. I flicked that freckle from time to time then I continued down until I was at the border of her bright red pubic hair. 'What's it called, an Aussie kiss?'

'Ohh.' She nodded and spread her legs wide. I licked her vulva, flicked at her hard clit and slowly deepened my fingers in her.

She gave a soft moan and shifted her hips.

I hadn't had so much as a grunt from her that first night in my apartment. I knew there was more than a passing chance I'd come within two minutes of entering her this time too, so I focused on my hands and mouth. It seemed hard to get her response to deepen. There was no pretending, I needed to prove myself. I wanted to prove myself.

When I touched inside her hip, at the narrowing of her waist, and the bottom of her butt, she gasped ever so slightly. Her bellybutton was supremely ticklish, and I was surprised that she accepted my lingering attention to it, her bright laugh filling the room. She moaned louder and louder as my fingers and mouth got to know her folds. Her eyes finally went wide, then her stomach clenched and her hips shuddered. Perhaps the most ideal abstraction of all: a beautiful woman's face in orgasm.

I closed my eyes to regain control after nearly having a spontaneous orgasm of my own. I opened my eyes and her wide arms welcomed me. She took my cock and guided it in. Caireann's warm hands, the comfort in her deeply dilated eyes, the way her thighs slid up and down along my legs kept me teetering on the precipice but I held it together. Another contortion crossed her face. I was now addicted to her face, rapt in pleasure. Never known for my self-control, I stopped pumping and rubbed her clit again.

'Your turn.' She had to push at my shoulder several times. 'Please?' I relented and lay back in her bed. She curled her fingers around the base of my rod and guided it into her mouth. The way her tongue swirled, rough then smooth then rough made it hard to keep my eyes open though I wanted to watch her. She rubbed my cock with her cheek and chin, her entire face. She took me as deep as she could go in her mouth again. She delicately, but firmly, squeezed my balls.

I shot so hard that, had her mouth not caught it, it would have splattered her headboard. She moaned loudly as she drank me, a fresh rapture on her face. I pulled her to my chest and her copious hair surrounded me like a weeping willow. She tasted of stale Guinness and fresh semen, strangely delectable. I studied the terrain of her back with both hands. Her left hand combed my hair. 'Thank you, Sven.'

'Uh … you're welcome.'

Caireann's long hair twisted around her face like rusted barbed wire. She lay curled on the far side of the bed and tossed restlessly. I crept from the room, gently descended the stairs and found some eggs and a hunk of nice cheddar cheese in her fridge.

I poured my meagre cooking skills into preparing an omelette as a modest 'thank you' in return.

'What are you doing?' Caireann stood at the threshold of the kitchen in a long robe. She clutched it between her breasts. I couldn't get a fix on her expression. I looked at the pan before me. Was I making it wrong? 'I – I'm sorry, hope you don't mind … I just wanted to … to try to … you know … make you breakfast.'

Her lips opened to that dimpled smile. 'I've never had a lad cook for me!'

'I hope I'll do OK.'

'You'll do great. Sorry if I seemed upset.'

'I should have asked.'

'It's OK.'

I started some toast. 'Anyway, thank you, Caireann.'

'For what?'

'You know, telling me about the dream.'

'You're a bright lad, and would have come around to it. It's like those reflections in the River Liffey. All you had to do is look up to see the real image clearly. I just lifted your chin.' Her eyes were so sad. Her lips smiled.

'God, I love how you put it.' She watched me in silence. I had to ask. 'What happened with that artist 'friend' of yours?'

'Long story.'

'Do I look strapped for time?'

She laughed. 'He said I was the perfect model, inspired him. Painted me over and over and over. I have no idea how many times. I posed clothed, nude, he did my face, my body, my hands, my feet, my breasts, my fucking left ear, but we never touched, you know, not in 'that' way. One night, he was painting a portrait of my face at my flat, I was fully dressed. He suddenly got naked, and stood before me. It seemed like he … was just giving himself to me. He was beautiful. It all just … happened.' She paused. 'It was great, but I never saw or heard from him again. He didn't even split up with me. The only thing he left was that painting, the one he did of me that night. I don't even know if it's finished …'

'Wow. I'm sorry.'

'For what?'

'Well … I'm … we're both Americans …' It was among the stupidest things I'd ever said.

She laughed brightly. 'I knew he wouldn't be staying in Dublin just as well as I know I'll never leave. Guess these things are never easy, no matter how they come out.' She looked at me. Fresh anger welled in her eyes.

'I remind you of him.'

She nodded. 'He was a strapping, handsome young man. Even blond.' She wiped beneath her eyes. 'You do look a lot like him. That was why I stopped at the mall at first.' She forced a smile. 'Lord, you turned me on. Maybe I figured I'd go to bed with you before you could break me heart.'

'I was a lousy lay.'

Caireann had just taken a drink of water and she spat it on the table. 'But he never, not even once, made me laugh.' She dried her mess. 'Thank you, lad, for listening. First time I told anyone about Russell. In a way, I feel like … you helped bring it to closure.'

'It's the least I could do.'

She complimented my cooking, I complimented her house. I took one last look at the painting in the little nook then went to the door.

'You need directions back to your flat?'

'I'm good.' We kissed gently. 'Good-bye, Caireann.'

She smiled. 'Good-bye, Sven.'

I felt like there should be more, but didn't know what. There was a big gap in me that I didn't know how to fill. I extended my right hand. She grinned and extended her left.

We shook left-handed.

It may have been that the images of the stars from the prior night painted themselves on the clouds in my mind, but I knew exactly where to go to get back to the River Liffey despite the consumptive grey that had taken over in the morning, and the twists and turns walking the prior night.

The next time I tried to paint, I found I had been completely wrong: knowing the truth had not been to its betterment. I painted plenty, but didn't like anything I did. My architecture seemed uninspired, so I went to abstracts. They were listless.

127

I set my brushes down and returned to some of the places I'd painted when I first arrived. The Georgian townhouses separated by the bright colours of the doors, united by airy, lace curtains. I could sense my inspiration. A row of old shops, and again I could sense my passion, but I couldn't really feel it.

I started to walk to Caireann's place a dozen times. I never even reached the river.

The glass ceiling suspended above the St Steven's Green shopping centre held me fast. Every detail committed in suspending this clear ceiling like the sky itself reminded me of the quote, 'the devil is in the details'. Paintings of architecture are about details. Not that I paint every one, far from it, but the key points must be present or implied. A keystone on an archway, the rivet on a junction of load-bearing beams. Omit a key detail, and your structure is left with floating elements; it loses credibility; won't hold the weight of helium.

By contrast, in the abstract, the detail can, and must, stand out, even demands to not be anchored. It invites the viewer to be the anchor. Disjointed eyes in a stylized upside-down face pretending to be the sun.

A dark freckle on a clear skin lip.

The grey sky above suddenly cracked with golden sunlight and as quickly was enveloped in grey again. So brief a moment I could only trap it in my mind and try to interpret it later. I felt that illusive spark, smothered before it could burn.

'That was pretty, wasn't it?'

The sound of her voice brought a warm rush up my spine. 'Beautiful.'

'I can see why you like it.' She looked around the mall. 'I waited for you to come by, started out a half dozen times for your place.'

I laughed. 'Me too.'

'What stopped you?'

The words turned in my head, and I knew if I opened my mouth they'd spew like a broken fire hose, so I composed myself, found comfort in her eyes. 'I'm not sure. Afraid you'd turn me away, that I reminded you too much of your artist friend.'

'Afraid that once you'd found why you had a fixation about redheads … I would lose some appeal.'

'No … I mean … maybe. I don't know.'

She winked. 'I worried I was an abstract in the River Liffey, more fetching in the reflection than when you lifted your eyes to the real me. I learned long ago that mysteries lost can lead to lonely days.'

'Do you really believe that?'

'No … I mean … maybe. I don't know.' She said it in a very good American accent.

I laughed. 'You should know by now that I like both the real and the abstract. Your artist 'friend', what was his name? Russell?'

She nodded.

'Russell was a fucking idiot. So was my mother.'

She reached between my elbows and my waist, curled her arms around my back and gripped my shoulder like an eagle perching. Her heart beat so hard and fast, I worried she might explode. I'm pretty sure mine did too, so I squeezed her waist and kissed precisely at that freckle on her lower lip. She relaxed and let me.

I eased into her mouth, and searched for the middle ground between the real and the abstract.

She opened.

About the Story

DUBLIN, THOUGH IT IS a city, and capital city at that, has much of the feel of a small town, and being as I'm a small-town boy by breeding, this only serves to endear her. She was the perfect setting for my protagonist, Sven, to begin to unravel the mysteries of his own quirks and artistic passions. I relate in many ways to Sven and his searching through the mysteries of his mind, though I'm a little further down that road than him. I've had my red-haired lady (with a blessed measure of Irish blood) to be my muse in creative adventures.

The beauty in Dublin begins with her people, and the character of Caireann is a bit of the city herself, sexy, wise, spirited and enigmatic. Like all who visit a place for the first time, Sven sees Dublin through different eyes than native Caireann, though she clearly loves her city. Still, his peculiar artistic vision of the city reveals to her a new perspective, as much as her more seasoned eyes begin to reveal to him the deeper things he didn't even know he was searching for when he came to Ireland.

The river Liffey both divides and unites Dublin, and her reflections are an artist's dream. The often sparsely rationed Dublin sunsets can be revelations unto themselves, difficult to capture, and more difficult to quantify. It is the combination of these images that ultimately anchored my story, *Abstract Liffey*. A sense of breaking away from something old, a sense of uniting with something new. The perceptible shift one takes when one has gone from the living room to the bedroom. Beyond the polished vases and lamps that one shows to the guests to the earthier, but no less beautiful, inner sanctum.

I suppose it has become clear that I think Dublin is a lady. She is indeed an enigma, both abstract and tangible.

I am fortunate to remain bewitched by her charms, and I am honoured to have *Abstract Liffey* included in *Sex in the City: Dublin.*

Peeping Tammi
by Kelly Greene

CALL ME PEEPING TAMMI.

What's that you ask?

The answer is simple: I get off on every opportunity to watch couples, or any other combination of people, or any single person doing anything sexual. My obsession started while walking the dog one sunny afternoon in Phoenix Park, just north-west of Dublin.

I had let the dog loose as it was over a mile from the road. Whenever my pooch, Darby, starts to act strange, like there is someone about, she always comes close to me. If a stranger comes in sight or within her hearing, she walks in front of me, and so closely she trips me up. That day, Darby came right back to me and plastered herself to my legs. I looked around and saw nothing. But as I walked on, I heard what sounded like a woman's voice making those unmistakable sounds of sexual pleasure.

Following the sound into the undergrowth, I spotted a man's backside pumping up and down, making some lucky lass happy. I hushed the dog to prevent her from barking and I watched this man plough his business into her business like he was a farming machine tearing up the ground. Good grief but was he horsing it in. I was mesmerized by the spectacle and felt my box immediately go wet. I was also a little jealous. And I wished it was me in her place.

When he groaned and was about to reach his climax, I tore myself away from the sexiest sight I had ever encountered and walked away quickly with Darby close at my heels. My blood ran madly and I told myself to relax and just get home. I went quickly to my flat in Stoneybatter and off came my clothes. And my fingers became that man's fingers.

I had the strongest, strangest solo orgasm I've ever experienced.

The image of those two in the woods haunted my mind for weeks. Every time I thought about them I got all juicy. I started to walk the dog more often and every day I would scour the woods hoping to see a repeat performance.

But it was several months before I found one; I spotted a car parked in the trees and noticed it was rocking in a telltale fashion, giving away the activity of the occupants. I moved in close, peeped through the window and saw a young couple. A molly was riding her man and her face was in full view. She had her eyes shut, so didn't see me as I crept closer, almost touching the car as it rocked gently on its suspension in time with her vigorous thrusts.

When she finally opened her eyes she smiled at me. She welcomed my presence.

When she eased off him, his flute sprung up and was pure horse meat. She knelt on the passenger seat and bent her head down, turning her face sideways to give me a clear view of her mouth as it devoured his brute virility. Her breasts swung low. As she watched me, she indicated that I should show myself and pull my skirt up.

I couldn't do it. As excited I was, it was just too much for me to expose myself in public.

But I stayed and must have watched those two for half an hour before another set of wheels pulled into the car park. I rushed home again to relieve myself. I lay on my bed, my clothes thrown about the floor from my eagerness to disrobe, and I pleased myself by recalling the images I had just witnessed. I let my fingers roam and enjoyed the sensation of the overflow that had seeped out of my pussy. Then I opened myself, stretched myself wide, and felt the cooling effect of the summer breeze wafting through the window.

I deliberately avoided touching my clit. That would have to wait. I wanted this arousal to last. I inserted just one finger deep into my saturated sex and made little circular motions round and round inside. My mind pictured that pretty young woman fucking her man, her breasts bouncing with each thrust. I imagined how she must have felt, deep into her *feke*, knowing that I was watching her every move, delighting in her theatre of sin.

How I wished it was me, not her.

I needed to be filled, to be loved just as hard as she had been. I would have loved to wrap my lips around his big red pipe, kissing and sucking him to climax. I would have taken every drop of his manliness; swallowed it all and then shown him the residue on my tongue before kissing him hard on his mouth, letting him taste himself, giving him a little of what he had given me.

This was getting good.

The first touch of my clit was expected. It is my finger, after all, but the impact of contact felt like an electric shock. I slipped a finger back inside the slippery depths of my sex. My cunt gripped my digit; throbbed and pulsated around it.

My bosoms needed attention, so I grip both my nips hard, making myself gasp with the pain and excitement of the sensations coursing through my body. Why do I love to make my eyes water by snagging my nips so hard?

I could wait no longer. One hand stroked across my flat belly and found my clit waiting patiently for its release. I rolled my finger round it until I could no longer hold back. Then changed my action to a vigorous rubbing motion, my orgasm only seconds away. My mind tripped back to that lovely *rosspot* bouncing on her pikey. As the climax hit me I imagined his tool buried deep inside me, my box gripping and squeezing him like it was trying to do to my fingers.

Autumn turned to winter and still no luck. I walked day after day in those woods trying to find another couple making love outside. It had become an obsession with me. I *needed* to watch.

And then on one exceptionally cold winter evening, I went back to the car park with Darby and found several cars parked up, as if waiting and full of bog warriors wanting to show off their sexual prowess. One of the cars had the interior light on, so I made a slight detour to walk closer to it.

A man and a girl sat in the front seats, snogging. I slowed right down as I neared the window, angling closer, making sure that if there was anything to see I wouldn't miss it. Alongside the car I stopped moving; this couple obviously wanted to show off. My feet, in fact, refused to move me away and my eyes fixed on the young man's hands as they pushed the front of the girl's T-shirt higher, until her white bust was showing clearly. She wore no bra. There was nothing except his hand to hide her wonderful young titties from me. He rolled her nipples around in the same way I love to handle my own. Moisture seeped into my knickers and I desperately wanted to touch myself.

Another car came into the car park shining its lights across me and the car I was watching. It scared me and I ran for the road. At home, in what was becoming compulsive behaviour, I stripped off my clothes and gave myself a huge climax.

When my husband came home, I reverted to the little housewife, cooking him some supper and watching television until bedtime. Did I mention I'm married? No? Well, I am. But I never really saw the television screen; my thoughts remained in the car park.

At the office the following day I simply could not get the scene in that car from out of my head and I began to hatch a curious plan.

After work, I ran straight upstairs and quickly changed from my office suit into some old jeans and a big sloppy jumper. I decided I would also wear a pair of boots that I used for gardening. Downstairs, I found hubby's long waxed cotton coat. When I wore it, the hem fell to my feet and effectively hid the fact that I was female. With this old baggy coat covering my curves, I resembled a small man.

I set out to *walk* the dog.

But the car park was empty.

I risked waiting around, knowing my husband wouldn't be home for well over an hour. But no one came. I was gutted; all that planning and nothing to show for it. My jeans were too tight to put my hands inside the pockets. I wondered why manufacturers bother to put pockets in girls' jeans; they are just about useless, especially when the jeans are as tight as I like to wear mine. Then it occurred to me that if I had been able to get a hand into a pocket, I would have also been able to touch myself between my legs. Not that it would do much for me that night, except frustrate me even further. But it made me think about what I might wear in future to facilitate such a thrill, because I was sure to find another car sooner or later with a couple in it who wanted to be watched.

I returned home disappointed, still thinking about ways to peep without being identified as a woman. After supper I spent some time looking through my wardrobe trying to find just the right pair of trousers, but everything I owned was too tight for my purposes; so tight that it was impossible to even slip my hand inside the waistband. I eventually came across an old pair of open-crotch tights that I had only worn once to thrill *him*. He liked that sort of thing. But they gave me an idea.

Sorting through my trousers again I found a pair of tight-fitting trousers that had been ruined by grass stains the previous summer. I went to my sewing room and, using the tights as a pattern, refashioned the trousers like open-crotch tights. Leaving only a waist band and four strips of material to hold up the legs, it left my entire crotch open and very exposed. Unfortunately the trousers were white so I quickly mixed some dye and changed the colour to a very dark blue: navy blue much like the sort of colour of trouser a man would wear for walking at night if he didn't want to advertise his presence. I washed, dried and ironed them and then I tried them on as soon as my hubby left for work. I stripped off my dressing gown, and, looking in the mirror, I pulled the trousers up and fastened them around my waist. I admired my work. I looked so damn sexy, only the slim pieces of material covering my otherwise naked bum. The holes at the back and sides were totally superfluous; I didn't need to open them up at all; that was just vanity.

Did I dare to go out wearing nothing but these cut away trousers under his old coat? I fetched it from the cloakroom and, standing in front of my mirror, I slipped it over my shoulders. Just a T-shirt covered my upper half. I had no bra because that would emphasize my bust and I wanted, for once, to hide my tits.

I fastened the coat to the lowest button, just below my knees, then stood up to see if it was obvious that I was not the man I pretended to be. My hand slipped into the false pocket, felt naked skin and sent shivers down my spine.

I walked out into my garden, still completely safe, but the sensation of having my pussy bare under the old coat made my skin goose. I wanted to leave the property and get into the woods, but I had to get ready for work so reluctantly went back indoors.

A quick shower and I set off to work. I hated every minute of the day; it seemed as if this evening would never come. I normally love my job in the centre of Dublin, but today it seemed so pointless and such a waste of my precious time; time that could have been spent looking for young couples in cars.

I raced home faster than I should have done. I hit ninety miles an hour along the by-pass in my eagerness to get home to those cut-away trousers and hubby's old coat. My heart was beating so fast, like a teeny Jenny on her first date wondering if she will give in to *him* and become a woman. I wasted no time on the usual cup of tea. Nothing was going to stop me now. I dashed up to my bedroom, stripped off my suit and my undies, and located the trousers hidden in the back of my wardrobe.

I pulled them up around my waist. I couldn't help notice the way they framed my *gee*, exposing it so nicely. My bum looked so round and cute and just as exposed. I felt and looked so sexy. I just knew this was going to be the night!

I wrapped my almost naked body in his coat; the hood pulled up over my head hiding most of my long blond hair. I called the dog and went out through the gate. It was as if I was someone else instead of the respectable house wife and career girl I had always thought myself. I felt like a tart; a brazen little trollop.

My hands were busy with the dog lead until I reached the woods. Then, as soon as I had released the lead, my hands went into the special pockets, both sides slipping directly onto my bare flesh. I could feel the heat emanating from my exposed cunny. I could even smell the aroma that only made itself apparent in the bedroom; that musky smell of a woman in heat, ready for whatever her man desired of her, wanting everything he has.

I cheated the poor dog in my haste to get back to the car park, only to be disappointed. Not a damn car in sight. I sat at the same picnic table, but this time my fingers had ample access to my hot wet bits. I had to be careful not to make myself squish. But it was so good being able to do this in a public place but feeling hidden from view by this big old coat. I waited for at least half an hour before the lights of a car pieced the gloom of the forest, searching as they swung around, coming to a stop only a few yards away from where I was sat. I prayed it was not just another dog walker parking his car. I realized I was holding my breath waiting to see what happened next, my finger automatically stroking the naked flesh hidden under my coat.

The interior lights in the car came on as someone opened the door, then the other door opened as well. In the dim glow cast by the small light I could just about make out a man and a woman. The front doors slammed shut, then the back doors opened and they both climbed in, onto the back seat. The back doors closed. The interior light faded and all was dark and very quiet.

Not wanting the dog to give me away, I tied its lead to the picnic table and crept toward the car. I was almost there when suddenly the interior light flickered on again. I stopped dead in my tracks. Had they seen me stealing forward to peep into the car? Was the light an indication of the door being opened, or was it, as I hoped, lit to reveal and exhibit what they were doing to any dirty old man in an old coat that happened to come along? Or in this case, a dirty young woman?

Frozen to the spot, I watched them sitting in the back and snogging like a couple of teenagers; his hands exploring the front of her shirt, the bottom of it coming open as he eased his hand further up, onto her breasts.

Creeping closer, both of my hands went to work inside the coat and worked on my wet lips, bringing me quickly and dangerously close to a climax. My feet crept forward of their own accord, delivering me closer to the pool of light surrounding the car until I was right against the side.

Her tits were naked; glowing white in the illumination of the interior light. His pipe, out of his fly, stuck up like a big red beacon. Her small hand was wrapped around it, making it look even bigger than it was. They were still locked in a kiss, oblivious to anything other than their desire for each other.

They broke the kiss and his eyes locked on mine. He smiled and whispered something in her ear and she turned her head towards me, smiling, telling me it was OK to look; it was their intention to give a show to whoever was lucky enough to be present.

My fingers were working overtime doing what I should have done in the private of my boudoir, not out

140

here in this dark and dangerous car park. They at least had the security of the car around them. I had nothing, not even the dog who was tied to the picnic table back at the edge of the woods. But the fear of getting caught just made the situation more exciting and my fingers responded by working even harder at bringing me off. I had to forcibly restrain myself because I shouldn't come. Not out here, it was just too risky.

He lifted his bum up as she pulled his trousers down; then her skirt went and she was struggling to get astride him. She managed to get herself on to his lap and he looked up at me as she slid down, impaling herself on his big hard cock. Her face was a picture of sinful lust as he penetrated her. He reached out towards me. My heart nearly stopped. I thought he was going to open the door, but he pressed the window winder and the window opened an inch. And he asked me to show her my cock. What the hell did I do now? My disguise had worked too well; he really thought I was a dirty lad.

Thank goodness my head was above the level of the roof so the light didn't shine on to my face. He would have seen the bright red of my blush as he asked me to expose myself to his loosebit. I had no choice but to ignore his request. I didn't have a cock to show her; all I had was a neatly shaved cunt.

Her hands locked behind his head as she rode him. She turned her head to peep at me. Her lips were red from their passionate snogging; her mouth slightly open in an inviting way. 'Please show me your flute,' she said.

Realizing I had a choice to either run or to expose my "flute", I reached down and undid the bottom button of the coat. The next button followed, then another. My fingers kept undoing the buttons. Until all of them were undone, and so was I. My heart was hammering inside my chest as I pulled the coat open, exposing my naked flesh to two complete strangers. Her gasp was completely audible outside the car because she saw what was under my coat.

His eyes popped. They certainly didn't expect to see a glistening wet smooth *gooter* staring back at them; nor did they show any sign of being put off by the fact I wasn't the man they expected. It was, in fact, quite the reverse. My fingers still poked through those wonderful holes in the pockets, stroking my so inflamed desire as I watched them go at it like hopping rabbits. The car bounced and she rode him to a climax. He grunted, stiffened and pumped her full. She was gasping with both lust and from the energy she was expending.

My legs almost collapsed from under me as my climax hit me so hard and from so deep down, it took all of my strength with it. I managed to hold onto their car to prevent myself from falling to the ground. My face touched the glass of the car window.

She opened her gobbler and vocally joined me in sweet shuddering fulfilment.

I then quickly buttoned up my coat and went to fetch poor Darby, tied to that table.

About the Story

I WAS AN EXCHANGE student in Scotland one year in college, but found myself heading over to Ireland and Dublin when I could. I felt more connected there, either because I'm half-Irish on my father's side (and his parents came straight from Ireland), or maybe because I like a dark pint of Guinness and James Joyce is one of my all-time favourite writers (go Molly Bloom!) I did spot a man looking into the windows of parked cars at a park there, and I thought: *Why are peeping toms always men?* Women like to watch too, maybe more so; but they watch behind closed doors, not in public. I've been fascinated with the motivation of the peeper; read Orrie Hitt's *I Prowl at Night* or *The Peeper* for excellent investigations of the kink. In certain ways, Hitchcock's *Rear Window* is about the urge to look into windows, hoping to see something tawdry and illicit.

I haven't been back to Dublin in ten years but I am planning a month-long trip in 2011. Maybe I'll stay. Anything is possible in that city.

With a Vengeance
by Sean Black

BY THE TIME I'D realised that Sinead was crazy, I was naked on the roof of the Gresham Hotel. A few hundred feet below on O'Connell Street taxis jockeyed for position and grim-faced commuters threaded their way home. Sinead, meanwhile, was backing towards the lip of the roof, her long coat open to reveal a black basque, her long black hair being blown in every direction by the swirling wind, her tongue darting over perfect white teeth as she coaxed me towards her as my momentarily proud erection shrivelled away in the freezing wind.

'Come on, Declan. What you afraid of?'

'Aren't you cold?' I'd asked her.

She let the coat drop from her shoulders. 'Yeah. That's why I want you over here. To warm me up.'

I took a step forward. Like I'd been doing, in one way or another, ever since I'd met her. Knowing that it was the last thing I should be doing, but unable to help myself. Not just because she was crazy, but because twelve months before I'd even met her, I'd changed her life for ever.

It was a dank Friday night in late November. The rain was bouncing off the road as I drove home. Surface water and fallen leaves made the surface slick. By the time I saw the man walking along the side of the road towards me, it was too late. A second later there was a thud and then for a fraction of the next second his face was staring at mine through the windscreen. Then it was gone as the windscreen shattered, and his body rolled over the top of the car.

I braked as hard as I could, the pedal tapping against my foot as the ABS kicked in. I blinked away the shock, but the spider-patterned glass in front of me did away with any illusion that I'd imagined what had just happened. I opened the door and stepped ankle-deep into a puddle of water.

The road behind me was quiet. No other cars. No cries of help. Nothing besides the sound of wind and lashing rain.

I worked my way back along the road. The numbness, the unreality of the whole thing was starting to ebb away, replaced by a rush of thoughts. I hadn't seen the man. I'd had no chance of avoiding him. But I'd had a pint after work. Two pints in fact. Shamefully, I was suddenly grateful for the silence.

Edging my way along the side of the road, I shouted into the storm. 'Hello? Can you hear me?'

There was no reply. Headlights appeared coming from the direction I'd been travelling. I waited for the car, a silver VW Passat to stop, but it didn't even slow down. In fact, if anything, it seemed to accelerate.

There was a ditch that ran parallel to the road. That's where I found him, one leg bunched up to his chest, the other splayed out. His arms were stretched out over his head. I climbed down beside him. As soon as I saw his face I knew he was dead. His eyes were open. His mouth was open too. I grabbed his wrist, and checked for a pulse. Nothing. My heart was pounding. His was stopped.

I stood there for a good few minutes. Hoping that someone would pull over to see what was going on and make the decision for me. None of them did. I counted off ten sets of headlights flashing past in either direction before climbing back out of the ditch, and getting back into my car.

I fumbled for my Blackberry and punched in 999, asking for an ambulance to come, saying that I thought I'd seen someone knocked down by a white van which had kept driving. They asked me to stay with the victim but I pretended like I was losing the connection and hung up.

Then, I drove home.

The accident made the news; a mention on the main news and a couple of follow-ups in the nationals before sliding down to the local weekly and disappearing from view entirely. There was an appeal for witnesses and mention of a white van. My lie's easy acceptance didn't make me feel smug, only more guilty if that was even possible. The fear of being caught gradually abated, replaced by recurring insomnia, a low-grade melancholy, and a spasmodic urge to tell someone. With the alcohol out of my system, I could have walked into any Garda station and told them how it had been an accident and how I had panicked. I'd probably have gotten a fine and a few points on my licence. That seemed inadequate, and, anyway, I wasn't looking for the slate being wiped clean or absolution. In truth, I didn't know what I was looking for other than to not feel the way I did.

A year to the day, I stood on the front step of the dead man's home. I had my speech to the man's widow all prepared. But before I could knock, the door opened. She had jet black hair and dark blue eyes. She was wearing a crushed-velvet dress which clung to her hips. There was a slit near the top of it which exposed the cleavage at the very top of her breasts. She noticed me looking and, rather than giving me the look I'd become used to from Irish women, that look that suggested I was beneath contempt, she smiled. She smiled and for that second I forgot why I was there.

'Can I help you?' she asked.

'Sorry, Mrs Byrne?'

'You must be looking for my mother,' she said, turning on her heel and walking back inside the bungalow. Unsure of what to do next, I stood there and watched her.

At the door into what I guessed was the lounge, she turned back round. 'Are you going to come in then or are you going to stand there staring at my arse?'

I stepped inside, closing the door behind me.

'What was it you wanted anyway?' she called from inside the other room.

From the moment she opened the door, what I wanted had changed. I wanted her, and I sure as hell wasn't likely to have her by telling her I was here to apologise for knocking down her father.

'I'm from the council.'

It was the first thing that came into my head. 'We're offering home insulation grants to the over sixties,' I said, stepping into the room where Mrs Byrne was watching television.

Mrs Byrne looked up, like she'd only just become aware that she had a visitor. 'Sinead, would you stick the kettle on,' she said to her daughter.

I spent the next half hour bullshitting frantically about this great scheme the council were running, and trying not to stare at the photographs of the man I'd killed on the mantle. There was no question of me confessing my sins now.

On the way out Sinead was waiting for me. 'You heading back to the office?'

'That's right.'

'Wood Quay?'

I vaguely remembered that was where the council offices were. 'Why? You want a lift?'

'Only if you're going that way.'

I should have made an excuse. Told another lie. I was practised enough by now. Instead, I opened the passenger door of my car. It was a new car. Brand new.

Sinead got in. 'Council must pay better than I thought.'

I got in the driver's side.

'Does this seat move back?' she asked.

I had to lean over her to get to the lever which moved the seat forward. At first I reached for it with my hand, mumbling an apology.

'Sorry, I haven't had anyone in the car until now.'

She took my hand in hers, her skin against mine. 'Here. Let me help you.'

She guided my hand to the lever. As the seat slid back she made a show of parting her legs.

Still clasping my hand, her fingers pushing into the spaces between mine, she guided my hand up her thigh and between her legs. The tips of my fingers brushed fabric first, then bare flesh. She was wearing stockings. The thought made me hard. Her hand pressed on, pulling aside the fabric of her panties. The hair around her pussy was smooth. Her lips parted as I pushed a finger inside. She was wet. A second finger joined the first and I moved up, massaging her clit.

'That's good,' she said, her eyes closed.

I looked through the gap between the seats, aware that her mother was still inside the house and might come out

148

at any minute.

'Maybe we should go somewhere?' I said.

Sinead's eyes snapped open. Her tone when she spoke suggested that desire had rapidly given way to irritation. 'What you scared of?'

'I dunno. Someone might see us.'

She stared at me. 'So?'

'Well …' I stammered.

She took my hand again, moving it away from her this time. She moved it so that my fingers which had just been inside her were against my own lips.

'Taste me,' she said.

The sudden rush of the moment had gone but I parted my lips anyway. The sweat from her cunt tasted like salt.

She dropped my hand. 'Do you live alone?'

'Yeah, yeah, I do.'

'Let's go there then. Or are you scared you might get into trouble with your boss?'

I'd forgotten about my lie. Going to my place would get me off the hook.

I drove – fast.

We never made it past the hall. The sex was frantic and aggressive. There was no pretence of making love. We were fucking. I was deep inside her, my tongue forced into her mouth. I tasted salt again. This time it came from my own blood as she nipped at me with her teeth.

When we were both done, we lay there, propped up against opposite walls. Her handbag was on the floor next to her. She opened it, pulled out a packet of Marlboro Lights and lit one.

She took a drag. 'You think I'm a crazy bitch, don't you?'

She wasn't any crazier than me. That was for definite. 'Takes two to tango.'

Her eyes flared with irritation again. She pointed the red hot tip of the cigarette at me. 'Don't fucking do that.'

'Do what?'

'Make it a joke.'

'I'm sorry,' I said.

'My dad,' she said, appearing to study me (although that might just have been my paranoia). 'He died a year ago today. That was why I was round checking on my mam.'

'What happened?' I asked her.

'Someone knocked him over when he was walking home from work. Left him for dead.'

I said nothing for a long while. She stayed silent too.

'Is that why you …?' I asked her.

'Why I wanted to fuck you?' she said.

I nodded.

'I have to go now,' she said, standing up.

She picked up her knickers from the floor and pulled them on. I sat there, watched her walk down the corridor, open the door and walk out. I sat there for a long time, wondering what the hell had just happened, trying to order it in my mind, and failing. Waves of guilt rolled back in. I'd gone to make amends to a man's widow, and ended up fucking his daughter.

I put my fingers back up to my lips and took a deep breath in. The low gnawing I'd felt in my stomach ever since the accident was gone.

But it would return, and so would Sinead; via a text telling me to meet her at the Gresham Hotel after work the following evening. I would do it then. I would confess.

But, unsurprisingly, the moment never arrived. Or rather, a drink in the bar was followed by an invitation on to the roof, and a dare-devil's fuck with half of Dublin passing by on the street below.

By the time the adrenalin rush had subsided, I'd resolved to let the whole thing go. To live with my guilt and get the hell out. But, as I ran through the usual platitudes in the lift, Sinead just smiled. 'We'll see,' she said, stepping out into the lobby and disappearing into the river of people on O'Connell Street.

It was one in the morning when the buzzer went. A week had passed, and the whole thing, my visit to the house, the incident in the car, the craziness on the hotel roof, had taken on a surreal quality in my mind. I stumbled into the kitchen, and pressed the intercom. 'Who is it?' I asked. But I already knew who it was.

I pressed the button to open the door downstairs, walked back into my bedroom and pulled on some clothes.

'You want to go for a walk,' she said as I opened the door.

'It's one in the morning.'

'You're only five minutes from the Liffey. It'll be romantic.'

It was true. My flat was only a stone's throw from the Quays. It wasn't anywhere you wanted to be walking at one in the morning. It was fine if you were heading home after a few jars. If you were on your way somewhere else in other words. But at night, even during the daytime, parts of the Quays were best avoided.

'OK, I'll go myself,' she announced.

I grabbed a jacket and threw it on.

We walked in silence down on to the river. Lights sparkled off the Liffey. She slipped her hand into mine as we walked. It was as if our relationship was moving in reverse.

Up ahead of us, I could see a knot of people, their faces shadowed by hooded tops and jackets. There were five of them; formless, genderless figures. They were making a show of messing, but that's all it was. They were aware of our approach.

'Are you not getting a bit cold?' I asked Sinead.

'No, I'm fine.'

'Maybe we should head back.'

She followed my gaze to the group. 'God, Declan, you're not afraid of those knackers, are you?'

She kept walking, and I had to run to keep up. Now we were maybe ten yards away from them. One of them turned towards us. He was in his early twenties with spotty pale skin and teeth like broken gravestones. 'Alrigh', bud. Got a smoke there?' he asked me.

It was too late to turn back. I shrugged an apology. 'Don't smoke. Sorry, man.'

'What about you?' he said, asking Sinead.

Sinead stopped and swivelled round on her heel. 'What about me?'

'You got a smoke?'

'Yeah, I do, thanks,' she said.

'Give us one then,' he said, his tone more aggressive.

I thought she was going to tell him where to go, and it was all going to kick off. But instead, she stopped, opening her handbag and fishing out her pack of Marlboro Lights and a lighter.

'Get ready to run,' she whispered to me, and my heart rate jumped another notch.

She tapped out a cigarette from the packet, and with a jaunty 'here you go' she stubbed it into the palm of the guy's hand. Before he had a chance to react, I grabbed her by the wrist and we took off. They shouted after us first – expletives, and threats tumbling out of their mouths. Then they came after us.

I didn't look back. I didn't dare. I just hauled Sinead along in my wake. A couple of streets along the threats fell away into the distance, and we slowed to a jog.

'What did you do that for?' I shouted at her.

She stared at me, defiant. 'What are you angry at me for? I just gave those little feckers a taste of their own medicine.'

The shouts started up again in the distance. Looking down the street, I saw the same group. They couldn't have seen us because they stayed walking.

'Let's get back to my flat before they catch up.'

Sinead blew a smoke ring in my face, then stabbed at the air, drawing a pattern with the red tip of her cigarette. 'That one that asked you for a smoke. I reckon you could fucking kill him, Dec.'

'Listen, I'm going home. You can come with me or you can stay here.'

She ground the cigarette under her heel. 'That's more like it. You're better when you take charge. Are you ready to take charge, Dec?'

I sighed. 'If we go back to my place, I'll do what you like.'

Fucking her from behind, I had a hank of her hair in my hand. She was screaming. I tugged at her hair again and she let out a guttural moan. She twisted her head round so that she was facing me.

'Hit me,' she said.

I stopped, the sweat pouring off me. 'What?'

She scrambled to the foot of the bed, then clambered down so that she was kneeling in front of me. 'Slap me,' she said, grabbing my cock with one hand and massaging my balls with the other. 'Call me a bitch.'

I hesitated. I was used to masochism in relationships. Hell, it was a key component of dating Irish girls. But normally I was on the receiving end.

'You said you'd do what I like,' she went on. 'Well, this what I like.'

'Being hurt?' I asked her.

'No, pain. I like pain. The pain takes away the hurt. Now, are you going to do it, or not?'

I didn't answer. What hurt was she talking about? The hurt that came with grief?

Glaring at me, she started to get to her feet. 'You're such a coward. Isn't that right, Declan?'

I pulled my hand back, and open-palmed, cracked her one hard across the face. Her cheek reddened.

'Harder,' she ordered.

I did. She must have moved her head because I caught her nose with the palm of my hand near the thumb. The blow drew blood from her nose. I stopped but she urged me on. She jerked at my cock, spitting out orders at the same time.

And I was lost. Lost in a world of guilt and remorse and despair. When I was finished, she got up, got dressed and grabbed her handbag. Her face was a right mess. The blood from her nose trailed down over her lips and on to her chin. One of her cheeks was swollen. A rim of red ran under both her eyes, the harbinger of two black eyes. Not for the first time in my life, regret came sharp on the heels of sex. I thought she was going into the bathroom to get cleaned up until I heard the door out of my flat close. I ran down the hall, looked out into the corridor, but she was already gone. I thought about chasing after her, but I wasn't sure what I'd say when I caught her. Exhausted, I fell asleep.

*   *   *

I woke to the buzzer, unsure of how much time had passed. I hauled myself out of bed, and clicked on the light, noticing for the first time the specks of blood on the sheets.

I clicked on the intercom button. 'Sinead?'

'Declan Riordan?' the man said.

'Yes?'

'Mr Riordan, this is Detective Sergeant Ross from Pearse Street Garda Station. I'd like to speak to you.'

You don't fully realise just how bad the phrase "she asked me to hit her" sounds until you're saying it in front of two stony-faced members of the Garda Siochana in a bleak interview room, with a solicitor putting his hand on your arm to get you to shut up.

'She was asking for it, Declan? Is that what you're saying to us?' DS Ross said.

'It's the truth,' I said.

'So what were her words exactly?' asked the female guard sitting next to him.

'Hit me.'

DS Ross and the female guard raised their eyebrows in unison.

'She liked pain,' I went on, digging deeper.

The female guard's face hardened. I didn't blame her. I placed my hands palm down on the table. 'Let me start from the beginning.'

My solicitor squeezed my elbow. 'I'd like a moment to consult with my client,' he said.

I shook him off. 'No,' I said. 'I want them to know everything.'

So, I did. I ran through the whole story all the way from the night of the accident. That part they clearly believed. I wondered if it was because I was admitting guilt rather than denying it. It was only when I got to my first encounter with Sinead in the car that more eyebrow raised glances were traded. In fact, DS Ross wasn't even trying to hide his smirk.

As I told my unlikely story, the pieces, the real story, started to fall into place. Sinead might have been genuinely crazy, her sexual tastes may have run broader, and deeper than mine, but I wondered now more than ever whether she'd known who I was as soon as I'd turned up on the anniversary of her father's death. I'd never get the answer to whether her setting me up for a rape charge was what she had in mind, or whether she'd simply decided that it was the best way to end our affair, Either way, it didn't matter. Not to the jury anyway. Sinead made for a hell of a witness. Butter wouldn't melt. On the stand the State's barrister didn't content himself with a knowing smirk. Instead, he went for the jugular, taking two crimes, one real and one imagined, and moulding them into something far more vile than the sum of their parts.

'I put it to you, Mr Riordan, that not content with killing one man, you then chose to visit evil upon the family he had left behind.'

I glanced over to the jury knowing from their studious avoidance of my gaze that now my life really was about to change. I closed my eyes, guilt replaced by terror at what lay ahead, and tasted Sinead's salty sweetness on my lips. It tasted like vengeance.

About the Story

I FIRST CAME TO Dublin in 1989 on a visit to a friend whose family lived on Collins Avenue in the city's north side. It was a very different place then; economically depressed, ravaged by heroin, a place people came from, rather than journeyed to. It was also, like my own place of birth, Glasgow, a city of tremendous warmth and resilience. It's a city whose greatest asset isn't construction, or flash cars, or any of the other bullshit accoutrements of conspicuous consumption that were so important during the years of the Celtic Tiger. No, Dublin's greatest asset is its people, particularly, in my opinion, those who live north of the Liffey.

In 1995, I moved my young family to Dublin from England. Flying back into Dublin airport from meetings in England, I experienced something I hadn't expected. For the first time coming back anywhere, including Scotland, I felt truly at home. Maybe I have an outsider's appreciation of the place, and it's that outsider's take which I brought to bear on this story.

The opportunity to write something for this anthology came via a blog written by a brilliant young Irish crime writer by the name of Declan Burke. Declan was helping draw attention to the fact that the publisher was seeking stories, and someone had posted in the comments section that writing a piece of literary erotica set in Dublin was too good an opportunity to pass up because "the entire paradigm of Irish male/female sexual relations is like a primer on S and M." The comment made me laugh, and then it made me think.

At the same time I'd read a thread in the *After Hours* section of a popular Irish message board which revolved around a seemingly perennial question related to why Irish men would be better off dating anyone but Irish women. Irish women, the person who started the thread contended, are difficult, high-maintenance, aloof and bitchy. I've always found them self-assured, funny, and, more than often than not, quite beautiful. But then, I'm an outsider.

On the other hand I've heard more than one Irish woman complain that Irish men are emotionally stunted, alcoholic, mammy's boys. There may be a grain of truth to that, but then Irish men don't possess the physical attributes to blind me to their shortcomings that Irish women do. Plus, what the hell do I know?

But taking these two archetypes, the cowardly male, and the predatory female, gave me a jumping off point for a story with my newly adopted city as the backdrop. I hope you enjoy it.

The City Spreads Startling Vast
by Elizabeth Costello

ALMOST THREE MONTHS PASSED before I ran out of money. In fact, it was coming close to the date when the length of time since Glenn's death was equal to the length of time we spent together. I sent the same text message to Joan and home: *I need a loan of €1,200.00*, followed by my bank account details for Joan. They knew well enough at that stage not to call. But the texts back were short. *We love you, and no*, my mother wrote. *Come home to us, or start working again.* Joan's said, *If I can't talk to you, I'm not lending you anything. Stop being such a silly bitch and come and stay with me.* A couple of hours later, she texted again with contact details of a friend working in a temping agency. No commitment, she wrote. And it's usually easy. I looked at my old friend, the crack in the corner of the ceiling. I could not figure out another way.

And so it was that on the Monday morning of the last week in October, I crossed the Portobello bridge for the first time that autumn. I felt like I did when, twelve years old, I went to school after they removed the cast on my healed arm. When I wanted to tell everyone that it was still broken, and could they please be careful. Still, I knew walking was a better option than the bus. Strangers I could handle, selling me my milk or delivering my crate of wine. But not when they pressed up against me. So I walked past the coffee shop where we once got spinach croissants, past the ladies setting up their flower stalls where he bought my solitary sunflowers, past the furniture shop where we put a down payment on a wooden bench. Our first joint purchase, never completed. All the way, leaves rained across the sky in great bursts, gathering orange and grey in raggedy-star bundles along the pavement. They danced around my boots and stuck to my knees and hem of my skirt. Branches of trees waved at me with their frantic limbs. The wind kept implying what a funny joke it would be to whip my hat from my head so I took it off myself and stuffed it into my bag.

'I've got something just about right for you,' said the woman in the office, smiling at me like I was five years old and this was my first day in school. 'Filing for a week in an accountancy firm. There's only three of them there, it's a quiet little place. Then we'll see how you feel.' She didn't even get me to do a typing test, barely glanced at my over-qualified CV. Joan must have told her the whole stupid saga.

My new place of work was in that part of town with the Georgian streets, the parks with their locked gates and no one inside, the perfect lawns and whooshing trees. I rounded a great, blustery corner on to their street. I pressed the buzzer and waited until the door opened and Denis, a man with huge glasses and no hair at all, stood there. He ushered me in to their office, where my job for the week sprawled higgledy-piggledy in one corner of the room, like a bonfire never lit. Tom and Philomena, still sitting at their desks, looked from me, to the mess, to me again. I figured there must be thousands of sheets of paper in there. There was a bit of an accident, explained Denis. It involved the cat and one of the old cabinets, he continued. From the way the others stayed silent, I guessed it also had something to do with him. All their files from D through to Y lay there (they didn't have any Zs). It would probably take more than the week to return everything to its proper home, and have each file safe and full in the new cabinet. But they'd see how I got on.

World became surnames, and letters and invoices, pastel yellows and pinks and greens, the new book smell of cardboard folders, and dust mites swimming in late afternoon sun. By the Wednesday afternoon, I was on M. The desire to get to Z by the Friday grew. An innocent one, but I wondered all the same at the adrenalin surge I felt on finishing each letter.

'Don't you have one of those white thingamebobs you want to listen to?' asked Tom on the Thursday, as I was getting towards the end of P. 'The nephew is about your age – he never takes it off.'

I thought of my iPod in its new home, the storage cupboard, along with spare light bulbs and Christmas decorations, old telephone directories, a bag of his clothes I'd found lying around the house. A T-shirt, two odd socks, a cardigan. I thought of his birthday gift to me of its 3,457 songs. I thought of the last time we listened to it together.

'I don't have one,' I said.

I went to the bathroom, where I slid my back against the door until I was sitting on the tile-cold floor, and pressed the soles of my hands against my shut eyes. I let myself sink into that memory. Our first morning in Honduras, waking on that half-filled air mattress on a wooden room in a tree, only a mosquito net between us and the sky. How I used the iPod to boom Tom Waits at him until he woke. How, when he did, he kissed my forehead and worked his way down, removing everything that interfered with his plan, such as a vest or pair of knickers. How sharp and hard his tongue grew, until I wrapped my hands around his ears and jaw and pulled him back up until we were face to living, breathing, contorting face again. How I then turned my back on him and pressed myself against him until his right hand was clutching my left breast and how then we were bobbing like a raft in a storm. How he pushed until I was face down in the sweat-filmed plastic and he was on top of me and together we reached the exact same place at the exact same time and how we rolled away from each other, laughing and sea-sick drunk. Before I knew what I was doing, my finger slipped beneath the hem of my trousers and underwear and was blurring up and down in there, until I was biting the thumb of my other hand and a moan still almost escaped me.

The next morning I did something I didn't know I was going to do. On my way to work, I stopped off at the bakery down the street from the office and bought four croissants. We sat around Denis's desk, where crumbs fell like golden snowflakes.

'Well, Ruth,' said Tom, a large piece of pastry clinging to the side of his mouth. 'We've got used to you about the place.'

'Stellar worker,' said Denis.

'A good girl,' nodded Philomena, in a voice that suggested she knew a bad one when she saw one.

It was almost five o'clock when I placed the final file, a Mr Joseph Williams, into the cabinet, in a pebble blue folder. I let the door slide shut and said, 'Finished.' Denis looked up and pushed his glasses up the bridge of his nose. He looked at me as though he'd never seen me before. Then he looked at the cabinet.

'Well,' he said. 'Would you look at that.'

Tom looked up too, wearing just the same expression.

'Well I'll be. Right on the dot.' Outside it was dark and a mist was falling.

Walking home that evening, the mist gave way to a wind-possessed rain that blasted my face and whipped off my hat once and for all. It seeped through the duffel of my coat, moving on past my cardigan and skirt, my tights and shirt and underwear. The skin on every inch of my body, except for my back, soon burned wet and cold. The rain pushed me against the door as I got the key in the lock and turned it. I half fell into the hallway, to face Frank coming down the stairs, his bag slung over one shoulder and his football boots dangling from his hand by their tied laces. His eyes widened as he took me in. He stopped walking, his open mouth threatening a smile.

'Hi Frank,' I said, as I drip-walked past.

'Well hello there. Wait a minute now, would you? How are you?'

His fingers curled around my elbow. I turned and looked into those water-blue eyes that peered back at me without blinking. I looked down at his fingers and his hand went to the banister, where they wrapped around that instead.

'It's just nice to see you out and about for a change,' he said, his voice higher than usual. 'You look more yourself than I've seen you look in a while.'

By speaking, he was breaking the rule I set the day I came back. When I explained how the only thing stopping me from ending my life was the fact that I could feel safe in my flat. Safe meaning left alone. The fact was, this was a lie. I never came close to wanting everything to end. It struck me for the first time how cruel that was of me. I could see it in his body posture, in the way his eyes flicked from my face to his hand on the banister and back again. In the way he still hadn't fully closed his mouth.

'Don't worry,' I said. 'I'm not about to jump.' I glanced over the banister as I spoke. I had to smile just so he'd know it was a bad joke. I knew then, that if I stood there any longer, his arms would be around my back, pressing me to him, and I would be smelling the scent of aftershave and mint and feeling his hot wet tears on my cold wet neck.

'So long Frank,' I said, turning and half running up the steps and around to my door.

'I'm off next week,' he shouted up at me. I turned, my hand still on the key in the keyhole. From this angle, I could see the top of his hair-stubbled head. I noticed it was cut tighter than usual, and how this suited him.

'Australia,' he said. He watched my face, waiting for me to remember.

'Australia. Of course.' He was going there for a year. 'Good luck Frank, if I don't see you between now and then.'

'Leaving do is Thursday night.'

'Have a good one.'

I passed that weekend in pretty much the same way I'd passed every day that autumn prior to my stint with the cabinets. I put on the television and left it on until the agency called Monday morning. Saturday, I spent a couple of hours on the treadmill in the gym across the road. I ate bowls of Cheerios and spaghetti with garlic and chilli fried in olive oil, topped off with grated cheese. I'd learned this recipe from my aunt in Italy and never got sick of it. There were five bottles of wine left in the last crate I'd ordered; I drank three of them. Saturday night's one I drank on the roof of the extension below my window, necking the bottle. Wrapped in a blanket, I looked at the stars and the small dense clouds moving across them. I stayed there even when a big one came and started spitting on the city. I could see Frank's window above, glowing a pale yellow, though I didn't see his shadow move across once. He was probably out. The only Saturday nights he was ever in were the ones when he threw a party. Starting with his housewarming back in the spring.

He lived in a bedsit, so we were all in the one room. I only knew the couple from downstairs and had just met Frank the day before. Some people were sitting or lying on the bed; the biggest group was standing around in the tiny kitchenette. Glenn was sitting on the arm of the couch, having an earnest-looking conversation with the couple. I had just come from a club and spent most of the night talking to Frank's college friends, the group in the kitchenette. It was only when daylight began to creep in through the curtains and I was finally feeling as though, if I lay down, sleep would come, that Frank came over with Glenn and introduced us. Told me how they met on a scuba diving course in Spain the year before. Laughter bubbled its way up through me when I took in his grave face and the steady eyes that appraised me; I couldn't help myself.

'Nice to meet you,' I said. 'Aren't you enjoying yourself very much?'

As soon as I spoke, I saw how I must have seemed to him: overly confident, too pleased with myself, arriving at a party where I knew no one and acting like its long-overdue life and soul. Then he said, coming closer as he spoke so that he was leaning over me and I could see the small damp curl that clung to his skin below his right ear and the way his eyelashes curled long and dark red and the freckle on his upper lip, 'I think we're enjoying ourselves equally.'

And then he grinned. A month later, he was staying in my place at least three nights a week. Three months later, we got on our plane to Honduras.

Monday afternoon the agency called again. Three days, but a bit hectic, I was warned. An estate agent that managed to stay in business by renting cheap accommodation mostly to students. It was on Baggot Street, where all the suit-wearing bagel-buyers throng the street at lunch hour.

'Thank you,' I said, surprised at how sincere I sounded.

The man behind the desk stared up at the new girl as the question barked.

'Who's got the keys for Harold's Cross Road?'

I didn't know. I stared back and said, 'Hello, I'm – '

'Marie, there's someone here,' he shouted, while putting on his coat. 'Where are the bloody keys for – '

A bunch of keys plunged through the air and through his sentence, past my left ear. They thunked against the wall and hit the ground. He glared at me as he went to pick them up and I took in the muddle of desks and phones and people behind where he sat.

That first day I spoke to no one, except all the people who phoned. I spent my lunch hour sitting on a park bench, where icy sun freckled through leaves, and coffee warmed my hands and sharped down my throat.

'How long are you here?' asked a blonde-haired girl at lunch on the second day.

'Just until tomorrow,' I told her.

'Until Denise gets back then?'

I shrugged.

'Well, if you're not doing anything, you're welcome to join myself and the girls for lunch. We're going to a great crêpe place around the corner.'

She smiled a shy smile. What could I do?

'OK, thanks,' I said.

We scraped chairs around the chrome table. I ordered a melted chocolate and banana crêpe with a strawberry milkshake. Outside the tourists and workers and shoppers ant-filed up and down. The girls began to talk and I had no choice but to listen.

'That's it girls. It is so over now,' said the one with the sparkly nails and spaghetti-thin eyebrows. They all looked up and gave a chorus groan.

'What happened?' asked shy blonde.

'I can't go out with someone who blows his nose every five minutes. That's what happened.'

'Come off it, Jenny,' said shy blonde.

'I am serious, Laura. Literally, in the cinema, every five minutes. No exaggeration. The guy's a hypochondriac.'

'So you dumped him?' asked the one sitting on my left. The one in the purple polo and matching lipstick, red hair scraped into a schoolgirl ponytail that perched on the top of her head like a question mark. Beneath it, an Audrey Hepburn face.

'I said I didn't have the time to be seeing anyone.'

'Sounds easy,' said Audrey Hepburn.

'I'm not finished. You know what he did? He started crying.'

The waitress arrived. Chocolate, dark and thick, bubbled over banana slices. Sweet and sweet. I gazed at it and breathed in. I sipped my strawberry milkshake, winking bubblegum pink. I forgot all about tears dripping into drinks. Then sparkly nails resumed.

'I said, look, Maurice.'

She looked around at us then. I looked up guiltily from

my freshly cut slice of chocolate dripping lunch.

'I said look. There is no point in you acting like this. I mean, it's not the kind of behaviour a girl is going to find attractive, is it?'

The girl who had not spoken yet gave an appreciative snort. She was a mass of softness and gentle edges in a deep pink sweater, her eyes kohl-smudged.

'Do you have a boyfriend?' said sparkly nails then. They all looked at me.

'No,' I heard my voice say.

'Join the club,' said softness. This time, I smiled to their laughter.

On the Thursday, sun got swallowed up by night-dark clouds and November soothe-scared us all afternoon with its drum blanket, on the roof, against the windows. Lonely streetlamps flickered on. Inside, electricity glared and voices flashed naked in the silence. I wanted to go up to the window, look at our sad reflections and at the darkness beyond. I wanted to be out there, walking the ghostly street.

'Are you doing anything tonight?' asked shy blonde at five o'clock.

'No,' I replied.

'Come out with us,' she said. 'We're planning on getting drunk.'

Seven Mojitos later, I went up to the guy standing at the stairs, watching the people dancing.

'That's a nice shirt,' I said. I meant it. It was plaid and soft-looking and mostly bright pink.

'Thanks,' he said.

'Where'd you get it?' I asked.

'H&M,' he said. He was looking at me with a bemused smile. It was a smirk more than a smile and I guessed he couldn't help it. He looked like the kind of person who was used to drunk girls approaching him. Like he already recognised it as a lucky perk he'd ended up with.

'You know the laneway between The Stag's Head and Dame Street?' I asked. And then I turned and walked out of there. I crossed the Liffey on the people-empty Ha'penny Bridge. I zig-zagged through a screaming hen night and the kebab munchers in Temple Bar. I crossed the long thigh of Dame Street, where the taxis waited and a drunk man muttered his way across in the opposite direction and the remaining leaves on the trees hissed and sighed. It had grown colder; the clouds were gone and the moonless sky stung with white-cold stars. He must have been right behind me all the way, because I was just in the archway, when his hand was on my shoulder.

'I'm glad your coat is such a bright red,' he said. 'I nearly lost you.'

'You knew where I'd be,' I said.

'This is true.'

He pushed his mouth against mine and I pressed the palm of my hand against the back of his head. My other hand opened the buttons of my coat. He tasted of beer and smoke and chewing gum. I didn't care how I tasted. His tongue pressed hard into my mouth, forcing my tongue down as it searched for something, along my teeth, the roof of my mouth. I pushed mine up until the tip of mine met the tip of his and we both pushed together, as though we wanted to separate, while our hands locked us together. All the time, his right hand moved fast and flat from my hip to my neck.

Behind me, the moss-green wall sloped inwards, offering up a slippery seat. I had glimpsed this in the second before he arrived and now I took a step backwards, pulling him with me. He lifted me onto it, his hands grasping the flesh of my rear, until my feet were hanging in the air, his body holding me there.

His clever hand tripped open the buttons of the cardigan, and then the shirt, of my demure office outfit. Then he reached back and undid the clasp of my bra. I wondered how often he had done this before. His hand rubbed hard and fast across my breasts and then his mouth was on one of them, then the other, sucking and biting my nipples ever so gently. Those are seriously soft lips, I remember thinking. More like what you'd expect from a girl. Before I had approached him in the bar, I went to the bathroom in a moment of inebriated focus, and threw my tights into the bin. Now, I pulled my knickers, a boring white cotton affair, off with one hand, lifting each foot lightly, as though I too had done this a hundred times. I stuffed them into my coat pocket. He yanked my skirt up until it was bunched around my waist. Just then, a group of men roared past on Dame Street. None of them, I think, looked in our direction. If they had, they would have seen the side profile of my thigh, and the left one of my respectably ample breasts, all nipple sharpened and standing white against the darkness.

To be honest, I had never had sex standing up before. But then, making a fool of myself had never mattered so little. I reached down and felt the hard bar of his cock and pulled open the buttons on his jeans and broke our kiss to look down. There it was, poking through. Looking up to say hi. I looked at his face and he was grin-smirking again, like it was all one great big joke. Which, of course, it was. I slipped from my perch in the wall and hunched down, put it hard and warm into my mouth, which moved up and down just a couple of times before I was back standing again. Now he wasn't grinning any more. In the quickest move I have ever seen, he went from not wearing

170

a condom to wearing one. Then his hands grabbed my rear again and I wrapped my legs around his torso, my arms around his neck. And that is how I found myself in the very early hours of a Friday morning, on a dark but not so tucked away part of the city, dancing hard and fast on the erection of a man I never met before. He was stronger than he looked, or at least pulled off an impressive feat for the occasion. I felt the world disappear. I became swallowed up by the growing sensation until it bubbled up and rushed out of my mouth in a groan. This made him move faster, until his rose, came up and out of him, and we were left panting as he pulled himself from me and let my feet rest onto the ground. I could feel the jerky beats of his heart and the shaking of his arms.

I kissed him on the cheek as he helped me close my buttons and fasten my bra. I left my knickers in my pocket as I walked away, still breathless and without anything to say anyway.

Walking after orgasm was a novelty. I took a long route home, one that took me on down Dame Street until I reached Christchurch. Then I went down Patrick Street, where the traffic never stops zipping or crawling, depending on time of day. I took a left at the church until I reached St Stephen's Green, where the trees swayed understandingly and not without a sense of humour. By then my breath had returned to normal. And all that was left was the coldness of my legs and the damp, bunched-up knickers in my pocket and the sensation fading back into where it came from.

I walked along the tramline, one foot right behind the other, like it was a tightrope. I met no one. See? I said to myself. Glenn is gone for ever. It didn't matter if I fucked strangers in the night-time. It didn't matter if I fucked

Glenn's Dad. I took out my phone, read again the text message sent by my brother James the week before I started temping. As I read, the desire to hit him, and hear the bone break, came back just as strong.

Mum's out of her mind worrying about u. I know ur sad, but u need to snap out of it. U only knew him 3 mnths. U know that's not even 1% of ur life so far?

But this time I deleted the message. And this time, I did not wish something worse than breaking bone: that it was James who had lain there in the morgue in Honduras, and not Glenn. Glenn, with his strand of his long red hair hanging loose, so that when they brought me in to identify the body, I knew it was him before they removed the sheet. And then they pulled it back anyway and there he was, only fatter. His nose, only purple and crooked. The man in the crumpled blue shirt and sad moustache told me it was broken, along with his lungs.

'Like that,' he said, clicking his fingers and shaking his head, the sad moustache turned downward in distaste rather than sympathy or sorrow. But Glenn had been a careful diver, I wanted to tell him. He had done all the courses and passed them with flying colours. Not like some of the backpackers who dive here because it's cheap, without learning how to do it properly, and risk their lives but manage not to die. Glenn only came here to see the fish that glow in the night time. He said it was like flying amongst the stars.

When I opened the red door that night, after walking the long way home from fucking the stranger, a couple was coming down the stairs.

'Is Frank in?' I asked them.

'Conked on his bed,' said the man.

'Anyone else in there?' I asked.

'Nope. You're a bit late.'

I got Frank's spare key from my flat and went across and into his. There he was, lying back-down on his double bed in the corner of the room, hidden torso down beneath the quilt and snoring. All of his things were gone, except for a bulging rucksack by the door, a pile of clothes on the armchair and party debris: wine-stained glasses, bottles of beer and cigarette stubs squished in saucers. I took off my coat and lay down beside him. I let my arm lie across his waist. When my phone rang, I woke dry and fuzzy in my mouth but with no headache at all. It was the agency. I glanced at the silver watch on Frank's wrist. 8.30.

'Sorry for the early call,' said the agency woman. 'But we need you in an advertising company off George's Street, by ten if you can make it. Basic data inputting this time. It's just for the day.'

Frank stirred but did not waken. I took a peek under the quilt and then threw it off. I slid down the bed along his Viking frame, using my elbows to lever me, and then put his morning-sharp cock in my mouth. I resisted the urge to look up when I heard the gasp, the 'Jesus', followed by the dry mouth whisper, 'Ruth'. I wrapped my lips hard around it and moved up and down, all the while my left hand wrapped around his upper arm. Then I straddled him. He closed his bug-big eyes and let it happen. I loved him briefly for that. Afterwards, I kissed his dazed face, his lips first and then his forehead.

'A goodbye gift. Thanks for everything. I promise you I'll be OK.'

An hour later, I walked past the tree skeletons, past corner shops and cafés, through doors and along the marble-floored reception area as though I'd worked there all my life.

'Marsh Advertising?' repeated the woman behind the

desk. 'That's on the seventh floor. Through the atrium to the lift. All the way to the top.'

I swung open a second set of doors and walked warm and tiny through the glass-roofed green. The lift carried me upwards, out-climbing the sun-craving palm trees and vines. At the top, a smile flashed at me behind a vast ash desk, across a sea of leather sofas and glass table tops.

'Ruth, is it? From the agency? I'll just tell Margaret you're here.'

I walked to the wall window. Below me and the empty blue deep, the city spread out startling vast. I pressed my forehead against the cool glass and stared into its jumble of houses and cars and streets as it filled to the horizon, all silver gleaming and morning new. I spoke his name – Glenn – to the morning, and told him, for the last time, I was sorry for carrying on.

Last week, I went to the graveyard for the first time since the funeral. There was no one else in sight. I placed a bunch of eight sunflowers on the earth's new icing of snow, one for each one he bought me. I had to scrape the snow off the temporary gravestone of a little wooden cross in order to see his name. *Glenn Garvey*. 'Ruth Garvey,' I said, and let myself cry, just a little. Snow glittered and above, the sky echoed it with blue. There was a blackbird singing in a tree behind me. And I could hear the wind, and in the distance, the traffic of the city sang to me until I turned and walked down the cemetery path, back towards the street.

About the Story

TEN YEARS AGO, I moved to Dublin city. At the end of the first year, a plan was formed among my flatmates to move to a bigger, better house in the 'burbs. I backed out at the very last minute. Instead, I got myself a bedsit in a Georgian house, walking distance from the city centre. Everyone, myself included, thought I was behaving rather foolishly. My new home, after all, was a dump. And I had no real excuse for this behaviour, other than the fact that I wasn't too keen on getting the bus.

Time passed and things changed, as they tend to do. I got a proper job and a proper place to live, one that had a television and a separate room for the bed and even other people living in it. In recent years, so many things have changed; I have found myself reliant on the bus for the first time since I moved here. Then, a girl called Ruth turns up in morning scribblings. She lives, of all places, in that old bedsit, a place I haven't thought of in years. She walks to her stress-free work.

Thinking about this now, it seems clear that the story came partly at least from a nostalgia for that part of town, and that stage of my life. But it's also about Dublin being the kind of place that comes right up and touches you, in the physical sense of the word. When things force Ruth to return to the world, almost everything she encounters rubs up against her in some way or another: the weather, cardboard files, men. It's what helps her to move on. Maybe moving into that bedsit wasn't so foolish after all. Sexy and ugly at the same time, Dublin is the kind of place to walk around in, as you let the weather beat you up a little and every now and then get thrown a shot like the docks at dusk or seagulls screaming over a beer-can-strewn canal.

Of Cockles and Mussels
by Stella Duffy

IF THERE'S ONE THING I know to be true about Molly Malone, it's that she was not sweet. Not sweet at all. She was wild and funny and exhausting to be with, she could be cruel too, had a mean temper and a hard jealous streak. But God she was good, to watch, to drink alongside, to play, to laugh, to fuck. And definitely more salt than sweet. Alive, alive oh.

I was sixteen when we met, she was already a grown woman of twenty-eight. Other women her age, the girls she'd been at school with – just for the few years before she started the business, set up her stall – the girls from her catechism class, dull, virginal girls all, she said, were long-married and on to their fourth or fifth babies by now. They spent their mornings shopping and cooking, their afternoons washing and cleaning, and their evenings moaning about mewling brats and stupid or nasty or lazy or boring husbands and interfering mothers-in-law; blaming the woes of their lives, not on the evil English as their husbands did, or on the lazy Irish as their landlords did, but on the priest that wouldn't let up when they dared brave the confessional. Not Molly. She had no quarrel with the Church, it didn't touch her and she didn't touch it, not since she was fourteen years old and Father Paul, on the other side of the confessional grille, had asked her to recount, blow by literal blow, the exact details of her afternoon down by the river with Patrick Michael Fisher. By the time I met her, Molly Malone went to church only on her favourite saints' days and no Sundays, and she had no intention of tying herself to a man, to a ring, to a child. No intention of tying herself to a woman either. More's the pity.

There's something about a woman whose hands are always a little wet, red from the cold and the wind and her own hard work. Her skin flushed with standing outside in all weathers, from morning after morning waiting for the fishing boats to come in, her hair pulled right back, scraped away from her neck, from her face, tied tight, held in, held away. Molly's hands smelled of the sea, of broken shells, what else could they do? But her hair, fat handfuls of thick, rich, dark brown hair, smelled of Molly alone. Of nutmeg grated on to warm milk, of the whisky added for a top-up, of the fresh pillow case – old linen, always ironed, no matter how hard her week – and of the warmth of her bed. Our bed. Her bed.

There was a song before there was Molly, my Molly. But after my Molly, that song only ever meant her.

Molly Malone told me she'd fucked James Joyce and he named Molly Bloom after her. Told me it was the bloom of her skin of her rose of her rising and falling and falling for him, in him, under him (through him in him with him) that is was and ever shall be. She took his hand and showed him where to go, how to go, how high to go, young artist falling from the sky on melting wings, into the melting Molly, wide bloom of melting Molly Malone.

She said she'd fucked Tristan Tzara too, when he was

over for a visit, before he and Joyce went off to Zurich together. Said his line about Clytemnestra on the quays of decorated bells was about her, Dublin quays, fishing boat bells. Molly was happy to fuck them, but had no time for their work – said it was easier when their hands were too full for a pen, their mouths too full for words. In her opinion there were too many Dadaist fellows anyway, not enough women, lads sitting in over-heated rooms and getting all excited about words when they should have had women to work for, women to please, no wonder their women turned to fucking each other. She was quite fond of Joyce, but thought the others were just odd, over-excited about all the wrong things. They could keep their poems and plays and prose, she was happier with a sentence that made sense, not the cut and paste variety Tzara preferred. Molly said scissors were for cutting hair, cutting bacon fat, shucking an oyster if there was no knife to hand.

I handed her a knife. She put it aside. Shucked me. Shucked off the plain and the hidden and the scared and the young and I grew under her tutelage, under her.

When we met. I'd gone down to her stall, I'd been there before, of course, many times. Middle child of five and all those boys, you know my mother didn't have anyone else to help her keep them clothed, fed, washed, clean. I hated doing the laundry, all that endless scrubbing of filthy boys' shirts and underpants. My brothers are not the only reason I started with women, but knowing a little too much about the ways of men certainly did make women a more interesting possibility when I was just sixteen.

So. I had been to her stall before, but I'd never met her, never actually talked to her. Molly Malone always had a crowd around her, a dozen housewives and as many stevedores, fishermen, passing clergy on occasion, they liked to buy from her because she always had the freshest and the best – my mother said she worked the fishermen for that privilege and I didn't doubt it – but also because she was so damn happy. It wasn't easy, back then, back there. None of us had anything to spare, none of us had time to give away either, not those who had their stalls in the fishmarket, or those who went to buy from them. I'm not talking the kind of *Oirish* poverty your American films like to revel in, all Fatima and famine, but the constant uncertainty, the grinding regularity of not quite having enough. Of never quite having enough. It's exhausting, and boring. It doesn't make for many cheery smiles or faux-folk songs breaking free from a mouth full of regular white teeth at the drop of a hat. For most of us, it was ordinary. And that's why people used to stop by Molly's cart.

I know she worked it, we all did, none of us thought her smile and her laughter and her smart, dirty mouth were all part of her nature, we all knew it was part of her work, and she worked it well. It drew her a crowd, kept them there while she told the story of the Kilbarrack fisherman she'd bought this cod from, the Howth girl she'd wheedled this tub of winkles from, the hard bitch at the end of the old harbour wall who hoarded the best oysters, brought in just once a week by her eldest son, and wouldn't let Molly buy any for her cart until she told her, word for word, about the last bloke she'd had. The oyster woman hadn't had sex for fifty years or more, but Molly could get a bucket of oysters from her with a twisted tale, whispered sweet.

Anyway, this day, a Wednesday, I arrived late. The baby brother was sick and our mother had had to sit with him while I did most of the day's work alone, which meant it was just tired bread and a thin soup for their dinner, and none of them happy about that, so our mother sent me out that afternoon to see if there were any leavings from the market, I'd sit with the boy and she would make up a stew of whatever I brought back. Now, I hate vegetable stew, it does nothing for my insides, and, even when I was a child, didn't agree with me too well, and scrag end of mutton can only go so far with a bunch of boys and my father, hungry from his wanting dinner. So I went to the market, to Molly Malone's cart. I knew she had to get rid of everything at the end of the day, and there were always plenty standing around to put up their hands when she offered this chunk of tired skate for half the price it had been in the morning, that bucket of fish heads and innards the nicer ladies asked her to remove, gutting her speciality and their relief.

This day though, I was too late. Molly Malone had given away the last chunks of tails and heads, all that was left on her stall were the blood and scales of the day and she was readying to pick up the cart and sluice it off, leaving it clean for the morning, gone six already, bells ringing for evening novenas, Molly was heading home to clean herself and sleep before she had to rise at four and grab the prime spot to meet the boats. (I assumed Molly was heading home to sleep. I know better now. I knew better not very long after.)

Molly Malone said later she could see it on my face, the anger, the frustration, the need, the hunger, the desire. I still believe she was making that up. What she could see on my face in that moment was simple damn fury that my stupid brother was sick and my stupid mother had sent me out to buy the worst food with the least money and my stupid life in which these kind of events were going to become more not less as I grew older, were going to become more difficult as I grew older and tried to have a family of my own, a life of my own. These problems were going to be my whole damn life. That's what I thought at sixteen, that's what scared me then. And yes, I did also think that Molly Malone looked good. And maybe I didn't even know I was thinking that. All I knew was she smiled at me and even though I was angry and tired and cold, I smiled back.

(I'd smiled at boys until then, and they'd smiled back at me. Tried more than just smiling often enough. Now I noticed that a girl could smile the same. Different. Better. The same.)

Molly Malone knew I needed what she had to give. She reached under the cart and pulled out a box. Inside were six of the shiniest, happiest looking mackerel I've ever seen. I shook my head, 'I can't afford that.'

'Yes, you can.'

'No, really,' she was smiling at me and it made me smile at her, smile even though I was confused and chilly and annoyed. 'I can't.' I reached into my pocket and pulled out the few coins. 'This is all I have, and I know my mother would want me to bring back some change.'

'You came out to buy fish heads and innards and wanted change from that?'

I shrugged, 'You can't blame me for trying.'

'No,' she agreed, 'So try this. You can take the fish, and keep your coins. I have a different price in mind.'

She nodded me closer to her and I took those steps willingly. I could smell the river now, and now the sea, the rocks and the waves and now the wide ocean bed. I could smell it all on her. And more. Could smell me on her.

I stood before her, she on one side of the cart and myself on the other. I was dizzy and interested and frightened and excited. I was sixteen.

She was speaking very quietly, and I had to lean in to hear her better, so many people around, other stall-holders, late like Molly, clearing up after their long day, shouting to each other, shouting to us too, laughing at us I thought perhaps, a few people pointing, one or two shaking their heads, a man called out 'there she goes, Molly Malone at it again' and another spat, calling after his friend, 'Damn me, how she does it, when I can't even get a bite.' I heard them, but I didn't hear them, because what Molly was saying was so strange and so unexpected and yet also so right, that I couldn't seem to take in what they were saying while I took in what she was saying. Asking. She was asking.

'So, it's a trade, a barter really. I don't want your coin, but I do want to see you. Naked. You take the fish now, and then later, tonight, or tomorrow, when you can get away, you come to my room – I'll give you the address, don't suppose you've been to that part of town too often, but you'll find it easy enough. You'll come to my room and you show me yourself. In your skin.'

I stared at her. 'That's all?'

She laughed, 'Isn't it enough for you?'

And I don't know where the bravery came from, maybe all those brothers, maybe the way she was leaning in, smiling, maybe it was just that I was sixteen, but I answered, 'Is it enough for you?'

She leaned back, folded her arms across her apron, the smile gone, her look as appraising and judging as ever it was when she stood on the dock and chose which fish to buy and which to leave.

'You're pretty enough, true. And you have lovely skin.

Nice hair when it's down I expect. But it's only six mackerel, child. Don't give yourself so cheap.'

I wanted to tell her I was my own to give as I saw fit, that I certainly was not cheap nor meaning to be, that she didn't know me though I knew her, we all knew her. I wanted to tell her so much. I said nothing. Held out my hands for the fish box and was off. She shouted the address after me. I wrote it in willing and kept it in my breast – from where it fell down to the pit of my stomach, the top of my thighs, the place between. And stayed there.

In any other family, a sixteen-year-old returning home with flushed cheeks and a full box of perfectly fresh fish might occasion a question about the purchase of those fish. Might even make other members of that family suspicious, would certainly urge them to ask how much exactly I had paid for the fish. Not in my home. I hadn't been in the back door a minute when two of the big hulking lads that, astonishingly, come from the same mix of flesh and blood that I do, were on me, one had me in a lock from behind, the other had taken a running dive at my feet, both of them pummelling me for not being home sooner, not providing their meal sooner. Then our mother was in the tiny kitchen as well, and the boys shooed out to join my father and their gut-clenching baby brothers – you'd think that lot hadn't been fed for a week or more – a chunk of bread handed over to make them quiet and a reach up to add a sharp-knuckled rap on the back of the head of the one a step older than me. I was standing so close to our mother he couldn't tell who had given him it, so though he turned and growled, he didn't dare hit back.

Then my mother was on the box, dragging it out of my hands and ripping the top off to see what was there. She wasn't quite as cool as the boys.

'Molly Malone gave you this?'

'She did.'

'Why?'

'I asked her.'

'You paid her?'

'I did.'

I lied.

And my mother knew I was lying. I wasn't sure what would come next, the lecture about Molly Malone's type or the back hand across the mouth or the fast hug our mother specialised in, the one that made none of her children ever feel left out, and none of us ever feel like we had enough of her either. What came surprised me. She smiled. She nodded. And then she shook her head.

'With all these men around in the house, I'm not surprised you wouldn't want a woman's company sometimes. I know I do.'

And even as she was speaking, she was lifting out pans and putting on the water, and handing me the knife for the potatoes and taking up a couple of onions herself.

We feasted that night. My mother could always make a little go a long way, but with a lot to start – she was a culinary queen. And my father knew it too, kissed her fondly before, during and after the meal. The eldest brother and I exchanged looks. The baby was only four years old and we'd all been glad of the break. The house didn't need another.

We had finished clearing the table, done with the washing up, the next-up brother had put the two little ones to bed, our father was reading to the older boys from the sports pages of the paper and I said to my mother, 'I might just pop out.'

And she didn't look up from the pan she was putting

away, just nodded, 'A breath of air?'

'Yes.'

'I'll not ask where you're going.'

'You can.'

I had my lie all planned, but she chose not to make me lie to her, she'd have hated that, spared herself the pain.

'I'll not.'

'I know what I'm doing.'

'I doubt that.' She stood up then, I could see her knees were hurting her, her back aching as it always did by this time of night, and then my father called from the other room, and already she was moving away, starting to go to him, heading for him as she always did. Our mother loved our father.

She stopped by the door, 'Do you want one of your brothers to walk you?'

'I don't.'

'Be careful.'

'I will.'

And that was it.

This is it.

I'm standing in Molly Malone's room – a wide, fringed shawl covers the window, another is thrown over her bed, a third sits on the back of the single chair. The shawls are of red and purple and deep green, they are the only colours in an otherwise bleached-clean room, floors and walls scrubbed pale, as if she never lights the fire in here, as if there is never any wood smoke or candle grease to mar the walls, the scoured floor. Maybe there isn't, it's a cool room. Not cold, but certainly cool. Molly Malone's room smells like driftwood, sea-washed day after night after day. It smells of clean linen. She has told me that beneath the shawl that covers her bed, the sheets and the

186

pillow-case are ironed. This is an extravagance of time and effort I can't imagine, but from the scent of the bed, warm lavender, I have to believe her. The room also smells of lemons. There is a wooden bowl of them on the thin table. One is cut in half. She is sitting on her chair and watching me, she is rubbing her hands, her fingers, her nails with the sharp flesh. She pours water from a cracked jug into a chipped bowl – there is the same picture of a courting couple on both – and washes her hands, wiping them down on her skirt. She has changed since I saw her in the market. She is wearing a clean skirt, no fish-blood or dried guts, a clean skirt, now with two long, dark marks from the wet hands, her own hands, down her own thighs.

'I'm ready.'

This is the third time she has said so. I don't know why I'm waiting, I know what I came here to do, am happy enough about it. I'm supposed to be shy about my own body, want to cover it, but in truth – other than from my brothers' prying eyes – I really don't mind. Never have. I like what I see in my small bedroom mirror a great deal, like it far too much I've been told.

'Look in that mirror any longer and you'll see the devil himself come up behind you,' our grandmother always used to say. She's dead now, and there is nothing behind me but Molly Malone's bed. The problem has not been that I've needed to shield myself from myself, rather that I've never been asked to show anyone else before.

I'm being asked to show now.

There are not many layers to remove. Once I decide to start, it is quickly done.

'And now I'm ready,' I reply.

* * *

It is so easy to be naked here. Cool, yes, but easy. I enjoy her gaze, am delighted to have someone else see this, see me, witness me. All of me. Her heavy gaze on my shoulders, my arms, breasts, belly – there – thighs, calves, feet – there – breasts, face – there. Molly Malone's eyes dip from my breasts to there, then rip back from there up to my breasts. I don't know if she's disappointed or delighted. Maybe both.

Perhaps both.

Both. Like me.

And then. Molly Malone naked. Five feet five in her bare feet, tired feet that stand all day, begin standing at first light, even in summer, waiting on the dock, tired splayed feet from years of hard waiting, and then the walk from the dock to the market, walking with her barrow, walking the cobbles and walking them hard. Molly Malone does not have pretty feet. Molly Malone naked and lying back on the bed, that back that has lugged lobster crates and crayfish pots, that has carried sacks of cockles and heavier ones of mussels, that back that bends and stretches all day as she reaches and weighs and parcels and sells. That back rests now, against the mattress and calls me, to rest on her. Molly Malone, reaching to me with strong arms. Upper arms with muscles delineated, Dublin streets have forged these muscles, forced these muscles, the old barrow with rutted wooden wheels pushed up and over, up and over, day after day after day (not Sunday afternoon, not Monday), upper arms strong enough to push from the dock to the market and back. Every day, twice a day. And her forearms. Molly Malone has fine dark hair on her forearms, shading the sinews that reach around the bone, embracing the tendons that years of shell-cracking, shell-piercing, shell-opening have made clear and sharp and strong. She does not have the pale skin of a lady, Molly's skin is mottled and freckled and lined, it is skin that has seen both sun and rain, skin that needs both sun and rain. Molly Malone has sold me sweet little crab claws with these good, strong arms, and I have been happy to watch her move behind the barrow, behind her apron, behind rolled-up sleeves. Now I watch her move on old white sheets.

It is night, there is no barrow, no market. We are in her room, and I am watching her, awaiting her. Her hair, which smells of clean linen, soft cotton, which is spread out across the darned sheet, across the thin grey blanket, beneath the coloured shawl, spread across me, her hair smells sweet and like night. It is night. She is not sweet. Her hands which, under the lemon, smell of soft shells ripped open, of mean claws tickled apart, of oysters smoothly shucked, of tiny shrimps tucked into perfect round pots, of fat grey prawns pinking with heat, her hands which smell of fish and of shellfish and of wide, wild oceans she has never seen, will never see, are on me. Molly Malone has hands that are wide and open and they hold me, I am both wide and open, full and ready. Molly Malone has hands that could clasp a small woman's waist or a young man's neck – hands that have done both – and now they clasp me, all of me.

This is the mussel. Open on the willing shell. We do not cook our mussels here. You can add your French white wine, your butter, your *herbes fines*, you may love your *moules marinières*, I'll take mine raw, and fresh, and from the shell. Dive in. I am the diver and I am the pearl. Tonight I search not the pearl, but the cockle. Small flesh, winkled out, called out. I call her out, my Molly Malone. In a while, a good enough while, she calls me back. And, calling to each other, we are one. A one that is made of three. One of her and the two of me. (We understand our trinities well enough in this city.)

Time passes. We spend many nights together, my Molly and me, and are happy to do so. My mother is happy too, relieved, I think. She always knew it would show itself one day, that I would have to show myself one day. If I was going to show anyone in this city it was safest I should show her, Molly Malone of the stories and the songs, Molly of the cockles and of the mussels. Molly who is not squeamish, who will gut and scale and rip and cut and open and taste. Molly who has always been happy to taste it all.

She did die of a fever. And no-one could save her.

But I'm not sure that many tried.

I tried. My mother tried too. Even the big brothers helped, and our father. Carried broth, brought cloths, lit candles. Prayed. Once or twice.

No-one could save her.

I left not long after, there was nothing for me there, not by then, not when so many people knew me as Molly's ...

Well, as Molly's.

And I have made a good life here. There is a wife. And children. The wife is pleased to be mine, though we must – of course – hide ourselves, dress up, dress down, dress to fit. I played the girl there, I play the man here. It works well enough, and my wife is happier that way, she and our children are safer that way. We are happy. Most of the time. And if I miss my home, if I think of that black port, or the land I have left, of the city I ache for sometimes, in truth, it is mostly the water I miss. The river, the docks, the sea. The smell of the sea on the wind. My mother and father are long dead, the brothers all married too, happily some, unhappily others. No surprise there. But sometimes, when the wife beside sleeps deep – and these hot nights in this hot land are too warm, so many nights when I long for a cool room, for a cold night – on those nights I throw off the bedclothes and I lie here naked, lie here showing all that I am. All of me. And I remember being seen, for the first time, for all of me.

Then a smile comes to my lips, and deep grin embeds itself in that place between my belly and my thighs, that place where I am both hidden and shown, where Molly Malone truly saw me. And here, in the dark, ten thousand miles from my childhood, more years than I can remember since that night, then hands that smell of a home I will never again see, touch me, take me, and hair that is washed walls and scrubbed floors and lemon halves and ironed linen fills my breath and my Molly Malone is as alive as I am. Lives as I do.

Alive.
Alive.
Oh.

About the Story

I'VE VISITED DUBLIN THREE or four times, each time for work, each time determined to go back again, with more freedom to walk, to explore, to sit around and watch. I've been to bars with journalists, to mass with a slew of elegantly faded elderly ladies (once a Catholic …), breakfasts with writers, and dinners with actors. I've drunk tea there, of course, and I've tried with the Guinness – sorry, it's still too bitter for this girl, even when it's at 'home'. For me, it's always been a very experiential place – about the eating and the drinking and the talking and the laughing. About the people I've met, and the ones I haven't. This Molly Malone is one I haven't met, but maybe wished I had. I didn't meet her in the old song that always made my sister cry when we were children, I didn't meet her in the pretty and chaste statue by the river. I may have met her in George Bernard Shaw's dark childhood house, Saint Joan standing alert in a dark corner. I probably caught a touch of her in Joyce's *Portrait of the Artist as a Young Man*, flying too high, heading for trouble and heading there anyway. I know she was hanging around Beckett's grave at Montparnasse, and maybe she picked up Lady Windermere's fan and fluttered it a little, giving Oscar an idea … all those men, writing about all those women. How lovely.

Doublin'
by Gerard Brennan

I WAS OUT OF my comfort zone, out of my depth and out
of my mind. She snaked an arm around my shoulder and
the side of her breast squished against my upper arm. Her
breath, a mix of Juicy Fruit and Coors Light, warmed my
face. She wore black lace underwear and a see-through
negligee-type thing. Her skin, and Jesus, there was so
much of it on show, smelt of a cheap musky perfume that
stuck in my throat and yet tickled the skin of my ball sac.

'Dance for you, love?'

She'd an English accent. Brash. Nasal. I guessed she
was from Manchester.

'That's right, sweetheart. I'm a *mad for it* Mancunian.
You having a good night? You Irish guys love to party,
don't you? What's your name?'

I thought about giving her an alias. Couldn't come up
with one. I tried to speak. Rasped. Spoke again.

'My name's Jimmy.'

'I'm Kylie.'

Kylie, my arse. I thought about the diminutive
Australian pop queen for a second. The Kylie with her
arm around my shoulder, sipping from a bottle of Coors,
had the blonde hair and cheeky smile, but there was
nothing petite about her. She was buxom, ridiculously
tanned and her eyes were heavy with porn star make-up. I

wanted to fuck her brains out.

She looked at me, looking at her, and ran her tongue from the base of her beer bottle, up the neck and did a quick little circle around the lip.

My face burned. I swept a hand across my brow, as if to blame the heat of the club.

'Hot in here, isn't it?'

'They have to keep us girls warm,' she said. 'Otherwise we'd all show up in cardigans.'

'Can't have that.'

Kylie took her arm from round my shoulder. I almost keened as the heat of her breast moved away from me. She wasn't going anywhere, though. Her hand traced my spine and came to rest at the waistband of my jeans. She hooked her thumb into the elastic of my boxers. A little jolt shot through my body. Curled my toes.

What the hell was I doing?

I looked to the bar. Benny had just been served. He'd a face on him like a slapped arse as he turned away from the barmaid, but it soon brightened when he clocked me and Kylie. I winked, attempting nonchalance. Probably closer to sleaze.

Benny scuttled over, quick-smart. Handed me my drink.

'What is it?' I asked.

'Dear as fuck,' Benny said. 'Close to thirty euros for a couple of vodka and Red Bulls? You may make it last.'

I sipped on the sticky liquid. Barely tasted the vodka. Extortionate prices and watered down too. I was suddenly conscious of my cash-light wallet.

'You don't come to a place like this to drink,' Kylie said. 'You come for a dance.'

A skinny brunette swept out of a dark corner and claimed Benny.

'Hiya, Danni,' Kylie said. 'Should we treat these two boys to a show?'

'If they're up for it,' Danni said. Her accent was pure Dublin. A local girl, then.

Kylie nodded at Benny's crotch. 'Looks like your one is.'

Benny laughed it off. Not a hint of embarrassment on his pretty-boy face. 'What kind of show, and how much is it?'

I kept my mouth shut, enjoyed the smell of Kylie. If Benny wanted to do the dealing, fair play to him. I'd developed a severe case of lapsed Catholic guilt. Well, maybe not *that* severe. I was still standing in a gentleman's club in Dublin city centre. It wasn't just the drink keeping me rooted in place.

'It's the kind of show you'll never forget,' Danni said. 'We get naked and intimate. Kissing, fingering and licking. Toys too. Fifty euros each.'

Benny glanced at me and I shook my head. I didn't have fifty euros.

'Fifty's a bit steep,' Benny said. 'Who carries that sort of cash around with them these days?'

Kylie picked it up, smooth as you like. 'Well, boys, as a special recessionary offer, you can get a private dance for just fifteen euros each. That's cheaper than a round of drinks, Jimmy.'

What could I say? It was my round.

'Benny, lend us thirty euros, will you?'

The music throbbed. Red light from the overhead spots cast Kylie in a cinematic and unreal hue. I sat straight-backed in a padded chair, legs spread as instructed. My arms hung straight at my sides. I probed the underside of the chair. Discovered punctures in the lining big enough

195

to slip my fingertips into. I wondered how many customers it took before it gave way under an excited grip. Probably not many. Watching Kylie dance and remove each skimpy item of lingerie, I imagined she'd blown many a gasket.

I moved my head so that her swaying body blocked the line of sight from the small video camera in the far corner of the room. The 'no touching' rule had been explained on the way in. One swift grope could end in a broken arm. Fair enough, I wouldn't touch, then. I tried to push away the thought of some lantern-jawed bouncer judging me from the monitoring room. Concentrated on Kylie's now bare breasts. They jiggled just inches from my face in time to a hip hop beat. I caught another strong whiff of her musky perfume.

She took a step away from me. Half-turned to show me her back. My eyes traced the complex black ink maze that was a tribal tattoo on her lower back. A tramp stamp, shaped to draw attention to a beautifully round arse. Her thong disappeared between her cheeks. Then she bent at the waist and rolled her hips. I caught a glimpse of the thin black gusset and gulped. This could only get better if she stepped out of her panties and rewound that roll.

She stepped out of her panties.

My hard-on propped the crotch of my jeans. Threatened to bust the zipper. I wished for tracky bottoms. Almost cried for them when Kylie lowered her soft arse onto my groin. She ground down hard. I was two thin layers of fabric away from penetration. My breath caught in my throat. Escaped with a little moan. Kylie laid back on me like I was the comfiest armchair in the world. She laid her head back on my shoulder. Gave me a birds-eye view of her huge boobs. Her dark nipples protruded like bullets. I ached for the taste of them. Salivated.

Hyperventilated. Damn near ejaculated.

Kylie slid off me and onto the floor. Turned and lowered her head to my incarcerated dick. For a fleeting moment I thought I was in for a blowjob. Was willing to overlook the camera in the corner for it, in fact. But she gave the flap of fabric over my zipper a little tug with her teeth then slid backwards on her arse. Her legs parted to give me one last peek of her shaved vagina. Then the music faded and she was on her feet. She tugged her underwear back on in jig time.

My balls ached, the tip of my dick niggled and my head throbbed.

I wanted another go.

Kylie led me back to the bar and disappeared into one of the shadowed booths. Benny waited for me at a fruit machine. It didn't look like he'd hit the jackpot.

'Well, how goes it?' I asked.

'I lost another fiver in this fucking machine. They'll have the administrators after me before the end of the night.'

'Been waiting long for me?'

'A few minutes. Mine cut it short after I whipped my lad out.' He pumped his fist to illustrate.

I gave him a smirk. 'You're a fucking eejit.'

'Wish I *was* fucking. No, I'm just an eejit tonight.' He nodded to the bar. 'Fancy another drink, bud?'

'Have you a hole in your head? The price of it in here. Jesus, no. Come on and we'll hit a club.'

'Fireworks?'

Fireworks on Tara Street. We were just about young enough to get into that place. Both of us were pushing thirty, but Benny had that young boy-band look about him. A bit like the little fellah out of Boyzone. Only straight. And alive. I was a little rougher round the edges, but I'd get away with a few more nights on the tiles yet.

'Yeah, we'll do Fireworks, then,' I said.

Slam. The whiskey hit my gut and the thick-bottomed tumbler thudded onto the bar top. Colour rose in my cheeks. I hated the taste. It left my throat sandpaper raw. But I was older than the Aftershock and Apple Sourz squad that jostled me for position at the bar. The amber firewater lent me an air of sophistication the young pups couldn't match. Even if it did churn my already sloshing stomach.

'Jesus Christ, Jimmy,' Benny said. 'Take it easy with the Jameson, all right? I'm not picking you up off the floor when you land on your ear.'

'Drink you under the table any day, son.'

Benny sipped at his Southern Comfort and lime. 'You'll be singing a different tune in the morning, bud. Mary won't let you lie on all day, you know.'

I feigned indifference but was all too aware of the clammy sweat that popped up on my brow. Benny was right. Yvonne would send the nipper in to bounce on the bed as soon as he got his breakfast into him. I checked my watch. After midnight. If I was lucky I'd be left undisturbed until eight in the morning.

'May as well be hung for a sheep as a lamb, Benny.'

'It's *hanged*, bud.'

'Fuck off and buy us a drink, *bud*.'

Benny ordered up a pitcher of beer and we grabbed a table that freed up. I could have done with another whiskey, but Benny was buying so I wasn't complaining. He filled the pint glasses – one part beer to one part foam – and raised his in a toast.

'Fuck the recession, we're on a session.'

I grinned and slurped from my pint glass. 'Good man, Benny. Good man.'

The construction trade had gone to shite and I was feeling the pinch. Benny the banker assuaged his guilt at being part of the economic problem – one of the many recipients of yearly bonuses and other benefits that killed our Celtic Tiger – by buying more than his fair share of drinks on a night out. I was happy to accept his charity when it was offered. He meant well, like.

A hip hop tune rumbled. Blood started running to my dick. It fattened. I crossed my legs.

'That's the song from earlier,' I said.

Benny poured another couple of beers. Squinted at me.

'At the other place.' The beat brought with it visions of Kylie's jiggling breasts.

It clicked with Benny. 'Oh, yeah. You might be right. All that new shite sounds the same to me, though.'

I half-listened to him and nodded. Most of my attention had drifted off to relive the memory of Kylie working her heavy hips. A coven of short-skirted clubbers drifted past our table. They left a lazy wave of musk in their wake. My dick twitched.

'I could really do with a handjob,' I said.

Benny edged away from me.

'Not from you, you buck-eejit.'

He looked to the floor packed with drunken damsels. 'Plenty of potential out there … you're married, though.'

'Yeah, I know. But sure, I'm only saying.'

'Well, fucking don't, all right?'

Benny looked like he was ready to square up to me. I thought it prudent not to remind him that he was the divorced one, not me.

'Mary's a nice girl,' he said. 'You should have treated her with more respect.'

Treat*ed*?

Benny shook his head and dug into his hip pocket.

'What about a whiskey this time?' he asked.

Treated?

Maybe I'd imagined it. Benny waved a note under my nose.

I snatched it off him. 'I'll go to the bar, then, will I?'

I faked unconsciousness for as long as I could but I had to give it up when I felt tiny fingers prod my eyelids. That freaks me out and Liam, our toddler, knows it only too well. I peered at him through crusty lashes. He gave me his cheeky grin and the urge to shout at him passed. It wasn't his fault I was hungover.

'All right, son?'

Liam giggled at my croaks. He tugged at the duvet. 'Mam-mam-mam.'

'Is your daddy up, son?'

My wife's usually soft voice crackled with an edge. The floorboards at the top of the stairs creaked and I'd a few seconds of mad panic and guilt. Had I said anything to her about Kylie? I didn't remember getting home so anything could have happened before I crashed onto the bed. She could have questioned a lipstick smear on my cheek, musky perfume on my clothes or a smug look on my face like a cat that got the cream. Shite, shite, shite. She'd come at me like a banshee.

I sat bolt upright, ready to defend myself.

'Jesus, you actually *are* up, then?' she said. 'I could smell the whiskey off you last night. Thought you'd be unmovable until noon at least.'

'Ah, Mary. I think I'm dying.'

She gave me a smile. A real one. Looked like I was safe.

'You've only yourself to blame, Jimmy.'

Usually I'd tell her to leave me alone, but for some reason I just took it and forced myself out of bed. I went for my dressing gown which hung off a handle on the wardrobe.

'Get away with that,' Mary said. 'You're not lying about all day feeling sorry for yourself. Get in the shower and sort yourself out. We've things to be doing today.'

I sounded a little grunt then hobbled towards the *en suite*.

'Thanks, love,' Mary said.

'For what?'

'Listening to me for a change.'

I was about to ask her what the fuck that was meant to mean, but little Liam grabbed her by the finger and asked for a drink. She rolled her eyes at me and let him lead her down the stairs. I flicked on the shower. The jets of water hissed. As I undressed, images of Kylie crowded my mind. I hummed the bass track to the tune she'd danced to. Got hard.

Locked the door.

Sweat rolled down my back. I pushed harder. Grunted. Cursed. Thought about Kylie and her shaved bits. Just to get me through the gardening, like.

I caught sight of Mary. She stood at the back door with a cold tin of Carlsberg in her hand. I shut off the mower, dropped the handle and trod across the freshly cut lawn.

'Go on, you good thing,' Mary said. 'You're putting your back into that.'

'Working through the hangover.'

'This'll help too, won't it?' She tapped the side of the tin with a short, practical fingernail.

I shoved my gardening gloves into my back pocket and

201

reached for the tin. Cracked it and swallowed a quarter in one gulp. God.

'You're a star, Mary.'

'No worries, love. Thanks for getting stuck in.'

I shrugged, worried that if I said anything I'd sound guilty. She must have taken it for modesty or something. Gave me a fond look. The sun popped out from a cloud and narrowed her eyes. Its rays picked out the auburn in her dark hair. She raised a hand to her head to shield her vision. It looked like a mischievous salute and went with her hipshot stance perfectly. A pretty picture.

'I love you,' she said.

'Love you too.'

And I meant it.

But if I loved my wife so much, why the hell was I angling for another night out? I came up behind her when she was elbow deep in soapy water. Wrapped my arms around her waist and kissed her neck. She stiffened slightly, which wasn't exactly what I was going for.

'Some of the lads are heading out tonight.'

'Oh?'

'Yeah … Em …?'

'I never got a lie-in last weekend.'

'I know, I know. You can get the next two Sundays.'

'That's big of you, Jimmy.'

I took the snarking. Savoured the memory of musky perfume. Relived the feel of a soft body, confident in its nudity, pushed against mine. The thought of another lap dance made my heart go whup-whup-whup.

'I'll bath Liam before I go. You get yourself a cuppa, right?'

Thawed her a bit.

'You owe me.'

I was cool with that. All I needed was this one night to set myself straight with my little obsession. Then I could get my head back into family life. I'd already tapped Benny for a wad of euros. No interest. With any joy, it'd buy me a happy ending.

Without a murky insulation of booze, the gentleman's club didn't seem so welcoming. The doorman jutted his jaw and sniffed in response to my friendly smile. He took my tenner and unhooked a frayed velvet rope to allow me access to the bar area. The clientele seemed subdued. Drunker than the night before. I hated the music. Big bass dance played through speakers too tinny to give it any balls.

But big deal, right? I didn't intend to stay too long. Just wanted to do the business with Kylie and leave. After that, I'd maybe call Benny and a few of the other lads. Ask if they wanted to meet me at Fireworks. See if we couldn't bang back a few shots and just end up where the night took us.

A small hand squeezed my arse. I looked over my shoulder. Danni. Benny's skinny brunette from the night before. I glanced over her head, into the shadowed booths. She prodded my chest.

'I'm down here, mister.'

God, her Dub' *gurrier* twang didn't do much for me at all. With her hair scraped back into a high ponytail, she looked worse than I remembered. And I wasn't that impressed by the memory.

Still, a little charm never hurt.

'How're ya, Danni? You look powerful. I was after a word with Kylie, though. She here tonight?'

Danni gave me a slow blink. Tried to place me. 'Oh,

yeah. I remember you. Your friend tried to get a free wank off me last night.'

Free? That was the worst of Benny's behaviour, then. He didn't negotiate terms before whipping his lad out. Maybe a couple of euros *could* buy me what I was after.

I asked about Kylie again.

'She's out the back right now. Sure why don't you buy me a drink while you're waiting for her?'

I looked around at the sad sacks with girls clung to them as they sipped on over-priced, piss-poor quality booze. Turned my nose up at them. But the wad in my pocket weighed heavy. What was the harm, eh? I nodded to an empty booth. Danni waved at the barmaid and held up two fingers.

'Send us over two bottles of Corona, Sammy.'

'I don't really like Corona,' I said.

'Trust me, mister. It's the best we have here. You definitely don't want anything from the taps.'

I sat with Danni and forced a few gulps of warm beer into me. She whispered a spiel into my ear while her bony hand traced my chest, my stomach and stopped short of my belt buckle. I kept my eye out for Kylie.

Then I saw her. She led a young lad with L-plates hung around his neck back to his mates at the bar. They cheered for him when she planted a little peck on his cheek. I told myself that it wasn't jealousy clenching my jaw shut. It was impatience. I just wanted to get what I'd come for and leave. And the more I inwardly repeated that little nonsense to myself, the less I believed it.

I nudged Danni. 'There's herself now.'

Danni sighed a little then patted my crotch. 'You know what you want anyway, mister.'

My balls throbbed. I got greedy. 'Yeah, I do. Why don't you call Kylie over, but stay with us for a drink at least, right?'

'I just don't do it, Jimmy,' Kylie said. 'Dancing and lesbian shows only. I'm not a whore.'

'Name your price,' I said.

She tilted her head. 'How many ways do I need to say it? I'm not going to suck your dick for money.' Her Manchester accent thickened as she raised her voice.

I sagged. Well, most of me did. The pressure in my boxers was not abating. And Danni's straying hands didn't help. She gave me a sharp squeeze.

'*I'll* suck it.'

'Thanks, Danni. But …' I looked pointedly at Kylie.

'What's the difference?' Danni said.

I shrugged.

Kylie fiddled with a beer mat, tore it in half and sighed. 'So you don't want a dance or a show and you don't want Danni to get you off. You've only eyes for me and my big gob, is that it?'

I shifted in my lumpy seat. 'Yeah.'

Kylie tutted and shook her head. 'Look, in the time me and Danni have been chatting to you, we could have done a couple of dances each. You're actually costing *us* money now.'

'Give me what I want and I'll pay you enough that you'll be able to knock off early for the night.'

Kylie's eyes pinged about in their heavily made-up frames. Her trout-pout twitched. I had her on the hook.

'Maybe we can work *something* out, Jimmy.'

It wasn't exactly what I wanted. Danni on her knees in front of me, with her mouth full. Kylie behind her, dancing to the same hip hop beat from the night before and blocking the camera's line of sight. Me holding on for dear life.

Kylie looked me in the eye. Smirked as she traced a fake nail around her nipple. 'Go on, love. Give it up.'

I grunted.

'Your cock's so *big*,' Kylie said.

Danni mumbled something that might have been positive affirmation.

Whatever she said, the sound waves made my dick thrum. I roared. Let rip. Kylie giggled and clapped her hands. The movement of her arms slapped her breasts together. I heaved again. Danni slurped and swallowed then slid back on her arse. Gave me a little flash before she covered her designer vagina with a delicate hand. A thin line of my semen dribbled down her chin.

I felt good and bad at the same time. Or maybe it was relieved and pathetic. Kylie didn't give me much time to analyse.

'Hurry up and put it away, for fuck's sake. I'm not going to stand here all night.'

I looked down at myself. Saw the state of my toppled erection and fumbled it back into my boxers. My jerky awkwardness drew a couple of snorts.

'Don't worry,' Danni said. 'It's not the smallest I've ever seen.'

Which, of course, implied that it wasn't anywhere near the biggest she'd ever seen either. The dirty bitch.

I watched them both get dressed with robotic efficiency. They went from naked to half-naked in mere seconds. The sudden change in the red-lit room's atmosphere did little to abate my self-loathing. I was a fool. A loser. Simply ridiculous. And I'd paid through the nose to feel that way.

'Let's go,' Kylie said.

'Can you leave me here for a minute or two, girls? Just

need a little quiet time before I hit the street.'

'Sorry, love. No can do. House rules.'

Kylie folded her arms, cocked a hip and waited for me to get up. I looked her up and down, noted the streaks in her fake tan and the patches of cellulite on her upper thighs. There was a certain sadomasochistic pleasure in deconstructing my object of lust. It diminished her for the sake of my pride, but it also needled me for thinking she was worth the desire. I figured the confused thought process was a sign that I was over her.

I slipped off the chair and made for the exit. Kylie led the way and let the door swing back on me and Danni. Rude as fuck, like. I shoved against the spring-loaded hinges and held it open for Danni. She brushed past me, stopped and turned on her heel. She produced a scrap of paper from God-knows-where and slipped it into my hip pocket, taking care to brush against my tender bits before she drew her hand back.

'Call me next time you need a little bit of relief, mister. I reckon you could do with something a bit more regular. You near blew a hole in the back of me head earlier.'

I woke early on the Sunday. Felt pretty good, too. I'd skipped the nightclub and spent a few hours walking around Dublin after my time with Kylie and Danni. Cleared my head out. When I got home, I'd slipped quietly into bed without wakening Mary. No awkward questions or unconvincing lies. Just a decent night's sleep.

I figured Mary had gotten up before me and was laid out in front of the TV with little Liam. The sheets on her side, though rumpled, were cool. I rolled into her spot and smelt her shampoo off her pillow. Breathed deep. I didn't lie for long, though. Needed to empty the bladder.

After a quick slash I padded down the stairs, thinking I

could get the kettle on before the nipper rushed me.

I almost stepped over the suitcases before I registered them.

Then I noticed the silence. Like, *really* noticed it.

I barged into the living room. Clocked the TV. Not even a glimmer of standby light. I scratched my head. Got the feeling. *Dread.* Tried to shake it off as paranoia.

I remembered the suitcases at the foot of the stairs.

It wasn't paranoia.

I went back to the hallway. Nudged one of the cases onto its side with an outstretched toe. It flopped onto the floor tiles with a hollow thud. I hunkered down and opened it. Empty. Except for a white window envelope.

The top of the envelope was ragged. Split open by a forefinger, most likely. There was no paper inside. I looked at the back of it. Mary's familiar scrawl in blue biro. It looked angry. Jagged and non-uniform. Big letters, small ones. Upper and lowercase. Hard to read. Except for the last two words: *Dirty bastard.*

Perfectly printed.

No *xox.*

I crumpled it and threw it at the front door. The little white lump fell short, so I picked up the empty case and launched it. I missed my target again, but took out a row of family pictures on the hallway wall. Glass skittered across the tiles. I could hear myself breathing like a phone pervert. Thought about Mary's note and grabbed the hall table from under the stairs. Sent it after the suitcase. This time I hit the door. Gashed the fuck out of the wood.

I pounded up the stairs and snatched my jeans off the bedroom floor. Upended them and shook them from the cuffs. My mobile and wallet slid out of the back pockets. I scooped up the phone. Tried to call Mary. She didn't answer.

After my third attempt to get though to her, a text message popped up on the display.

Pack ur shite n get 2 fuck!!!

'Ah, Jesus.'

I phoned Benny next.

'What do you want, Jimmy?'

'Was it you?'

'Me what?'

'Mary's gone.'

'I know. She's here.'

'Did you tell her …?' I replayed what he'd just said. 'Here where? At *your* place?

'You're a stupid fucker, *bud*.'

Benny cut the line. I stared at the 'call disconnected' message. It faded to black.

I'm a little slow, but I figured that Benny had told Mary about my little adventure at the gentleman's club. My first one, at least. As if the cheeky bastard wasn't there with me. And he was using it as an angle to get into Mary's knickers? Not that I could tell her that Benny was with me. Had *led* me there, in fact. Sure I'd only be talking myself into a deeper hole. For fuck's sake. The stupid bitch.

I wanted to get angry all over again. Knew I had no right.

I dropped my mobile onto the bed. It landed beside my wallet. I picked it up and flipped it open. The little scrap of paper with Danni's number on it was tucked into a corner of the note compartment. I hooked it out and unfolded it.

OK, I'd been no angel. But my best friend and my wife? Did shite like that really happen? Maybe I should have accepted it as karmic retribution, but my immediate thoughts were far from noble. I had the remainder of

Benny's cash, which he'd never see again, and a contact to help me reach new lows.

I tapped Danni's number into my mobile. Wondered if she could get in touch with Kylie on a Sunday.

RIGHT, YOU'RE NOT GOING to believe this, but I got the idea for this story after a good friend of mine told me about his first visit to a lap dance club. Yes, that old chestnut. Last year, my *friend*, who is the same age as me and is also a happily married man, visited a club with some friends on a stag night and treated himself to four private dances. And he thought it was great craic. Now, this friend of mine is a pretty sensible guy. Decent, like. I was pretty surprised by the fondness of his memories as he related his experience over a few pints. And get this – *he told his wife all about the four lap dances he bought.*

I said, "You told your missus?"

He nodded. Smiled.

I needed to know more. "And she said?"

"What else would you do at a lap dance club?"

That impressed me. Both my friend's honesty and his wife's blasé attitude.

But it got me thinking. What if my friend wasn't quite as honest? What if he knew his wife wouldn't have been anywhere near as laid-back about his confession? What if …? That question is a writer's bread and butter.

So I sent my character, Jimmy, to a Dublin club and made him a nastier piece of work than my friend. And I got him to take the whole experience way too seriously. Tried to present him as unhealthily intrigued by his first dancer. I pretty much explored the extreme opposites of all my friend's reactions.

As to the setting, I've been to Dublin loads of times. Love the place. It's ancient but snazzy. The people are slick but homely. And the nightlife? Phew.

I set a scene in Fireworks in honour of a terrific night I had there when I was still young enough to fit in at a nightclub. I drank too much, met the president of Ireland's daughter (never thought to buy her a drink) and got escorted off the premises when I fell asleep on my feet. Legendary. I still smile when I think about it. It was only a matter of time before I jotted down a little memento.

Author Biographies

Colin Bateman is a novelist and screenwriter, originally from Bangor in Northern Ireland. His first novel, *Divorcing Jack*, was published in 1995, won the Betty Trask Prize and was later turned into an acclaimed – at least around his house – film. He has written twenty 'quite good' selling novels, and also five books for children. He has recently embarked on a new series of crime thrillers based in a real life Belfast bookstore, No Alibis. The first of these, *Mystery Man,* was selected for the Richard and Judy Summer Read, and the sequel, *The Day of the Jack Russell,* has recently been published by Headline and is currently being developed for television. Bateman also created and wrote the BBC1 series *Murphy's Law* starring James Nesbitt and has the distinction of having written the only episode of *Rebus* not to be based on an Ian Rankin novel. He was one of the few living authors to feature in The *Daily Telegraph's 50 Crime Writers to Read Before You Die* and was named in *The Times' 100 Masters of Crime*. Despite this his wife still shouts at him when the dinner isn't ready on time.

Shelley Silas was born in Calcutta and grew up in North London. Her stage plays include *Eating Ice Cream on Gaza Beach* (NYT/Soho Theatre), *Falling* (The Bush Theatre, Pearson Writer-in-Residence), *Calcutta Kosher* (Southwark Playhouse, Birmingham Rep, Theatre Royal

Stratford East), *Mercy Fine* (Southwark Playhouse, Birmingham Rep). Her plays for Radio 4 include, *I am Emma Humphreys*, *The Sound of Silence* (short-listed for the Imison Award), *Ink*, *Calcutta Kosher*, *Molly's Story in Celluloid Extras*, *The Magpie Stories* (devised and co-wrote), *Collective Fascination*, *Nothing Happened* (with Luke Sorba). She adapted Hanan Al-Shaykh's novel *Only in London*, and Paul Scott's *The Raj Quartet* (with John Harvey). Shelley has written a television film for Touch Paper TV, *The Wedding Dress*, and compiled and edited the short story anthology, *12 Days*, published by Virago. She has written and performed specially commissioned short stories at the Cheltenham Literature Festival and the Hexham Book Festival and has contributed stories to *Little Black Dress* and *The Flash*. She is currently developing a TV comedy series (with Luke Sorba), which has been optioned, and writing a new play for Radio 4, *Mr Jones Goes Driving*.

A fine art graduate, **Severin Rossetti** taught the subject in Liverpool for a number of years before becoming disillusioned with the career. He now works as a gallery attendant for National Museums Liverpool, a job which leaves him poorer financially but much more contented and with time for thought. Coinciding with the switch in career, a similar dissatisfaction with what passes for *art* led Severin Rossetti to turn from painting to writing. Since doing so, and being drawn to the erotic genre, his work has been published in the UK by Black Lace, Forum and others, while in the USA his short stories and novels are currently represented by e-book publishers Renaissance Books, the most recent publications including *Shackled Maids*, *Faustina's Pet* and *Masoch's Domain*.

Ken Bruen has 26 published novels

Ten awards for the Jack Taylot novels

Three movies of his books completed in 2009

Have been receiving a lot of acting roles recently

Has a Ph. D in metaphysics and that's just simply to confuse people

Nikki Magennis is a highly strung incurable Romantic (with a capital R). She lives in rural Scotland and is sometimes a writer, sometimes an artist, and since late 2009 also a mother. Since her first erotic novel, *Circus Excite*, was published in 2006, she has written over twenty short stories and another novel. You can find her work in anthologies from *F is for Fetish* to the *Mammoth Book of the Kama Sutra*; including *Hurts So Good* and *Love at First Sting* edited by Alison Tyler and several of the Black Lace Wicked Words anthologies (*Sex in Public, Sex with Strangers, Sex and Music*.) Her latest novel, *The New Rakes*, also published by Black Lace, is a tale of sex and sex and rock and roll set in Glasgow. Nikki particularly loves writing 100 word fiction and her short pieces appear in several erotic anthologies from Cleis Press including *Pleasure Bound*, *Frenzy* and *Playing with Fire* edited by Alison Tyler. You can read more of her work and find out more at her blog: *nikkimagennis.blogspot.com*

Maxim Jakubowski is a twice award-winning British writer, editor, critic, lecturer, ex-publisher and ex-bookshop owner. He shares his time between the wonderfully dubious shores of erotica and the perilous beaches of crime and mystery fiction. He is responsible for the *Mammoth Book of Erotica* series and the *Mammoth Book of Best British Crime* series, is editor of over 75 anthologies and counting, as well as being the author of two handfuls of novels and short story collections. He was crime reviewer for *Time Out London* and then the *Guardian* for nearly twenty years, and also makes regular appearances on radio and television. He also co-directs Crime Scene, London's annual crime and mystery film and literature festival, and runs the MaXcrime imprint. *I Was Waiting For You* is his latest novel.

Though based in London, he has been known to travel and frequent hotel rooms with depressing regularity, which no doubt inspired his *London Noir*, *Paris Noir* and *Rome Noir* collections, as well as the *Sex in the City* series. He has lived in, or regularly visited, every city featured in the *Sex in the City* titles published so far. When not writing, he collects books, CDs and DVDs with alarming haste.

Craig J. Sorensen has been crafting stories since before he could write. In the thirty years since he left the small American country town where he was raised he has been fortunate enough to live in a number of fascinating places and meet people which have fed these creative endeavours. By day he is an Information Technology professional – a career geek. By early morning light continues to hone his love for storytelling and poetry. A musician and visual artist, he seeks to fuse these other artistic expressions into his written works as well. His varied erotic stories have appeared in print magazines and anthologies internationally as well as numerous online publications. He recently completed *Augsburg Diary*, an erotic novel that draws upon his experiences while stationed at a US Army military intelligence unit in West Germany during the early 1980's.

Visit Craig online at: *http://just-craig.blogspot.com/*

Kelly Greene has worked as a dancer in Portland and Seattle, a cocktail waitress in San Francisco, and a Feng Shui consultant in Los Angeles. She currently lives in Cardiff-by-the-Sea in California. She has stories forthcoming in several anthologies from Cleis and Harlequin, and a novel forthcoming from Harlequin, *The Next Wedding*. She is working on her next novel, an erotic thriller titled 69.

Sean Black was born in Glasgow, Scotland. After leaving school at the age of sixteen, he went back to college to finish his exams, eventually winning a place to study Philosophy, Politics and Economics at St Hugh's College, Oxford. During this time he also worked as a freelance journalist and published his first short fiction alongside fellow Scottish writers A.L. Kennedy and Irvine Welsh. Figuring that there might be more money in screenwriting than novels, he went on to study for a Master of Fine Arts in Film at Columbia University in New York. Five years after graduating, he finally got his first paid television job, writing for the iconic British television soap, *Brookside*. After nine years writing television drama, he started work on his first novel. Inspired by his experience of training as a bodyguard in the UK and Eastern Europe, *Lockdown* was bought at auction in September, 2008 by Bantam/Transworld. The paperback of *Lockdown* is due to be published in July 2010, alongside the hardback of its sequel, *Lock Up*. Both novels are set in the United States and feature ex-military bodyguard, Ryan Lock.

Elizabeth Costello is a short-story writer living in Dublin city. The journals *Southword*, *Loch Raven Review* and

Glossolalia have been kind enough to publish her stories. An Arts Council grant recipient, her work has also been broadcast on Irish national radio. In 2008, she was shortlisted for the Sean O'Faolain International Short Story Competition.

Stella Duffy was born in London, grew up in New Zealand, and has lived back in London since 1986. She has published twelve novels. *The Room of Lost Things* and *State of Happiness* were both long-listed for the Orange Prize. *The Room of Lost Things* won Stonewall Writer of the Year 2008. She has written over thirty short stories, including several for BBC Radio 4, and won the 2002 CWA Short Story Dagger for *Martha Grace*. Her eight plays include an adaptation of *Medea* for Steam Industry, *Prime Resident* and *Immaculate Conceit* for the National Youth Theatre. In addition to her writing work she is a performer and theatre director. Her latest novel is *Theodora* (Virago, 2010).

Gerard Brennan lives in Northern Ireland, with his wife, Michelle, and their two children, Mya and Jack. His fledgling novel-writing career is represented by Allan Guthrie of Jenny Brown Associates. He is not ashamed to beg and has been successful in two bids for funding from the Arts Council of Northern Ireland in the last two years. No mean feat in the current climate and something he is fiercely proud of.

He has written a screenplay, titled *The Point* (thanks to NI Screen for their funding and development guidance), that he intends to send to every production company he can find. The stage play co-written with his father, Joe Brennan, titled *The Sweety Bottle* has been picked up by a West Belfast production company and (if funding allows) it might just make it to the stage in 2010. On the side, and to preserve his sanity, he writes short fiction.

And he runs a blog dedicated to crime fiction in Northern Ireland, *http://www.crimesceneni.blogspot.com/.*
Sleep is no longer an option, so pass the coffee, please.
www.gerardbrennan.co.uk

More titles in the Sex in the City Range

Sex in the City – London
ISBN 9781907106226 £7.99

Sex in the City – Paris
ISBN 9781907106257 £7.99

Sex in the City – New York
ISBN 9781907106240 £7.99